THIS IS
the STORY
OF
You

Beth Kephart

CHRONICLE BOOKS
SAN FRANCISCO

Library of Congress Cataloging-in-Publication Data:

Kephart, Beth, author.
   This is the story of you / Beth Kephart.
      pages cm
   Summary: Seventeen-year-old Mira lives in a small island beach town off the
coast of New Jersey year-round, and when a devastating superstorm strikes she
will face the storm's wrath and the destruction it leaves behind alone.
   ISBN 978-1-4521-4284-5
   1. Hurricanes—New Jersey—Juvenile fiction. 2. Islands—New Jersey—
Juvenile fiction. 3. Survival—Juvenile fiction. 4. New Jersey—Juvenile fiction.
[1. Hurricanes—Fiction. 2. Islands—Fiction. 3. Survival—Fiction. 4. New
Jersey—Fiction.] I. Title.
   PZ7.K438Th 2016
   813.54—dc23
                                    2015003765

Manufactured in China.

Design by Jennifer Tolo Pierce.
Typeset in ITC Giovanni.

Page 19: Kolbert, Elizabeth. *The Sixth Extinction: An Unnatural History.*
New York: Henry Holt, 2014.

Page 84: Savadove, Larry and Margaret Thomas Buchholz. *Great Storms
of the Jersey Shore.* New Jersey: Down the Shore Publishing, 1997.

Page 226: Joyce, James. *The Portrait of the Artist as a Young Man.*
New York: B. W. Huebsch, 1916.

Page 235: "Pelorus Jack." Lyrics by P. Cole, music by H. Rivers.

10 9 8 7 6 5 4 3 2 1

Chronicle Books LLC
680 Second Street
San Francisco, CA 94107

Chronicle Books—we see things differently. Become part
of our community at www.chroniclebooks.com/teen.

For my father, brother, and sister,
and in loving memory of my mother,
my grandmother, and Uncle Danny.
Once the beach was ours.

PART *One*

1.

Blue, for example.

Like the color the sun makes the sea. Like the beach bucket he wore as a hat, king of the tidal parade. Like the word *I* and the hour of nobody awake but me. I thought blue was mine, and that we were each ourselves, and that some things could not be stolen. I thought the waves would rise up, toss down, rinse clean, and that I would still be standing here, solid.

I was wrong about everything.

In the beginning it was just the beginning. The storm had no name. It was far away and nothing big, mere vapors and degrees. It was the middle-ish of September. Empty tables in restaurants, naked spaces in parking lots, cool stairs in the lighthouse shaft, no line for donuts, deer in the dune grass, padlocks and chains at the Mini Amuse, the Ferris wheel chairs tipping and dipping.

The beach belonged to Old Carmen and the campfire nobody stopped her from lighting—four logs and a flame and the sea. The beach belonged to the retrievers and the one collie and the mutts who limped behind, yapping like they thought they could someday take the lead. You could watch the sky, and it was yours. You could stand on the south end of the barrier beach and see Atlantic City blinking on and off like a video game. You could ride your wheels home, and the *splat splat* on the wide asphalt was your sweet siren song.

Everything calm. Nothing headed toward crumble.

2.

September, like I said. Middle-ish. Skies so sweet and so Berry Blast Blue that Eva and Deni and I and the rest of us at Alabaster were taking most of our classes outside, our Skechers untied and our bodies SPF'd cloud high.

Science was bird-watching in the dunes. English was Trap the Metaphors. History was lessons on Pompeii under the shade of the schoolyard tree. Math was Algebra 2 taught at the picnic tables whose splintery legs were screwed in tight to the concrete pad in the school's backyard, the school that looked like a bank because once it *was* a bank, the big, round, metal eye of its abandoned vault still in the basement.

Our liberty projects were our Project Flows—our four-year independent studies. Water: that was the category. Subtopic: anything we chose. *Monsters of the Sea. Vanishing Cities. Shore Up. Glaciers on the Run. The Murder of Mangroves.* We chose our topics. We wrote our books. We understood that on graduation day we would leave those books behind.

Let the process define you.

Our principal, Mr. Friedley, was mayor material, this guy with fresh ideas who believed in straying from the path. *We learn wherever we open our eyes.* That was his motto. *Know the possibilities.* He said that, too. *Don't give up on the future. Give everything you have. Know who you are. Go forth and conquer.* We were six miles long by one-half mile at Haven. We'd conquered the place infinities ago.

We were The Isolates. We were one bridge and a few good rules away from normal. We were casual bohemians, expert scavengers, cool. *Woo-hooo,* we said, when the last Vacationeers drove off, over the bridge, Labor Day Monday. *Rumble rumble. See you next May.* And then out we'd come with our Modes, which were yard-sale vintage, to take back what was ours.

Eva's Mode was a 36-inch Sims Taperkick that she'd decoupaged-out with Betty Boop; that skateboard could fly—Eva's three braids going up and down on her back, each like a stick on a marching band drum. Deni had a Gem Electric golf cart, circa 1999—a cute little two-seater that she'd painted gold as the eye of a tiger. Gem was a gift from Deni's uncle. She drove it everywhere, slipping her aviators to the top of her head, where they remained, like a helmet. Deni even swam with those glasses on. She wore them in the rain. She walked around with two pools of reflected sky on her head.

My Mode was a pair of old-time roller skates whose clanking key I wore at my neck like a charm. It was the prettiest jewel you'd ever seen, that key. It left a bruise on my chest from all the thonking, a proud purple thing.

I'm medium everything—blond, built, smart. But with that key and those strap-them-on adjustables I was such pure speed that Eva would say, every fifth or seventh day, that I should pack for the Olympics already.

Yeah, right, is what I said. Yeah, right. I'm not going anywhere. Because I had my business in Haven. I had *responsibilities*. I had my mom, first of all—long story. And I had a brother, Jasper Lee, who needed me. Seven years younger and perfect, except for one thing: The kid was born with no iduronate-2-sulfatase enzyme, which means he couldn't recycle mucopolysaccharides, which is another way of explaining this lysosomal storage disease called Hunter syndrome, which is why his face is shaped the way it is, and why he has trouble walking, and why he may be losing his hearing and his seeing and I can't help it if you've never heard of it before, because there are only maybe a few thousand people with Hunter in the whole wide world. My prime business in Haven concerned my brother, Jasper Lee, who was Home of the Brave to me, whose disease I knew all the long words to, because knowing the names of things is one small defense against the sad facts of reality.

Mid-September, like I said. Outdoor classes, mostly. Old Carmen watching the flickering sea, the moon in the water, the flames around her campfire logs—all sizzly. Old

Carmen, a Haven legend: Someone should have done their Project Flow on her. Sitting like a sea lion on her patch of sand, the long line of her fishing pole tossed to the waves, a bucket at her side to help with the catch. Some people said Old Carmen was an heiress. Some people said she was outer space and alien. Some people said she was old. Vacation season, she disappeared. Labor Day through Memorial Day, she was present. Always the same age, the same clothes, the same fishing line, the same bucket. Old Carmen was Old Carmen. We just let her be.

I lived in a seaside cottage. I lived in the attic room on the topmost floor, my own private deck looking out toward the shore, a sliding door between me and the weather. This is how I'd copped a front-row Old Carmen seat and how I was first to see the dawn exploding and how I was the one for whom the dolphins came, slicing their fins through the waves, those dolphins like excellent friends, scientific name: *Delphinus delphis.* I was the first to see the bubble edge of the surf, where the baby clams and blue crabs and foraminifera (ten thousand kinds of foraminifera) sucked back into their hiding after the waves had knocked them through.

Monsters of the Sea. That was my Project Flow. That was me. I was on a first-name basis with the strange and lovely things. Kingdom through phylum through family, genus, species. I was the taxonomy queen.

I had the attic, which was two stories up, and the sliding doors that opened onto the crooked deck, and the deck itself. That deck was like a continental shelf. It stood on four pole legs, tossing a shadow across the yard below, a place we called the Zone. Every part and parcel of the attic and the deck had belonged, once, to my aunt. The tartan blanket, the drainpipe jeans, the penny loafers, the Marilyn Monroe tees, the faux tuxedo jacket, the curio cabinets, and the curiosities—all hers, once, just as the cottage, once, had belonged to my aunt, until she left it to my mother. "Over to you, Mickey," my aunt had said, according to legend, but I never knew for sure. I was in utero at the time.

Mickey inherited the cottage. I inherited the view, which is to say the sea and the sky, and the day I'm talking about had been spectacular, the air that kind of blue that snaps a shine into the sea and makes every speck of sand look like combusted mirror dust. Jasper Lee had set his alarm for a 7 a.m. he'd never honor. Mickey had been awake before that. I'd been up since five, watching the toss of the sea.

Out on the beach, the news was playing on Old Carmen's radio. The line off her pole glistened like a strand of dental floss. There was a mutt up to its belly fur in a slow wave, and the sea was behaving itself. There are 140 million square miles of ocean in this world. The oceans are mountains and craters and hot vents and tectonics and all their uncountable creatures. That morning, I was pondering a time when there was no sea at all, billions of years before now. I was imagining the earth all hot and blustery, all feisty and flames, working like heck to cool itself down, but mostly spewing its hotness like a cauldron. The sea covers seventy-one percent of our planet, but it wasn't here at the planet's start. The sea fell from the skies—any Alabasteran writing any Project Flow will tell you that. The sea arrived (most of the sea, that's how they teach it here) when the iced comets cometh, when the asteroids tore through the skies and shattered. The sea around us fell down upon us. It took billions more years before we showed up ourselves.

The sea comes and the sea goes.

3.

At school it was fourteen of us in the Class of O'Sixteen—give or take, less is more. Maybe where you're from they need three buildings skirted out with parking lots (students to the right, teachers in the shade) to accommodate the up-and-coming citizens of the world. Not in Haven.

First of all, we had our Modes, or else we walked. Second of all, the old bank they'd converted into our school fit us just fine. Into its basement (south to the vault's gloomy north), they'd carved a cafeteria that equaled Gym that equaled Arts and Music that equaled Study Hall or, also, Assembly Hall. On the three upper floors, in tall, pilaster-peeling spaces, they'd arranged four classrooms per. First grade through fourth: Level 1. Fifth grade through eighth: Level 2. Ninth grade through twelfth: Level 3. Sometimes we could hear the kids on Level 1 singing their Duck, Duck, Goose. Sometimes, from Level 2, the reverbing of *Of Mice and Men.* Sometimes Mr. Friedley would stand at the bottom of the spiraling central steps with the hole up through the middle and roar: *Go forth and conquer*. History was ceaseless in the repetition of itself. We lived with a severe case of déjà vu.

Except: On this particular day, when the weather was so revved full of allure that classes migrated to the exterior world, there was the dawn of something new. It was homeroom, just after the bell. We had already pledged our allegiance.

"Class," Ms. Novotny said, a new guy standing by the door. "This is Shift."

The guy turned his head inside his hoodie. He crammed his fists inside the pockets of his green-and-purple madras shorts. He slapped the heel of one flip-flop, then *slapped slapped slapped* toward the single extra chair, sat his long self down, hood still up, eyes averted. He was a transfer from someplace, but nobody knew where. He'd come by way of the bridge, unless he'd come by way of boat; there was no big reveal. He had a slim spiral-bound notebook in his hand and a uni-ball Roller clipped to the peak of his hood, and maybe Shift was his first name, or Shift was a trick name, and maybe he wouldn't be staying for good, but I felt sure of this: We'd never seen him before.

"Hey, Shift."

"Hey, yeah."

"Cool."

Eva's eyes like anime.

Deni with a calculating stare.

Me pondering the one word, *Shift*. Class? Order? Family? Species?

First period was birds by the dunes. It was Ms. Isabel already down in the lobby, her long cotton coat hanging past her anklebones, the lavender sleeves rolled to her elbows, a fat dahlia stuck in the current of her auburn dreads. Ms. Isabel was a big believer in songbirds. She said *tanageroriolevireothrustwarbleryellowrumpnorthernwaterthrush* like it was all one word. She hauled her science books around in a saggy roller cart, tucked the cassette deck into her purse, sank extra batteries into her pocket wells. "Listen," she'd say. "Identify." Making as if birdsong was Spanish, the only second language actually offered at Alabaster.

I was good, far more than medium good, at naming all those birds.

Birds were Ms. Isabel's dinosaurs, her dreams, her proof that it was our privilege to save what could still be saved of our world. "Every feather counts," she'd say. "Every song." Ms. Isabel taught activism by way of appreciation. Respect. Preserve. Study the signs.

On the day that Shift showed up, Ms. Isabel was waiting on us in the lobby for the after-homeroom bell, waiting and not looking up through the aperture in the spiraling stair, not watching us single-file out of homeroom and down the Level 3 hall and toward the marble stairs worn to a thin shine by so much climbing. The jingle bells around Becca's ankle went first. Marco and Mario—tallest and shortest, Filipino and Italian—went next, then Dascher with her brand-new anchor tattoo, then Deby, Becca's skinny twin. Then Taneisha with her platform wedges and her arm full of bracelets that jingled louder than Becca's bells. Then Chang with a fluorescent disc in her backpack's pocket—Chang, captain of Alabaster's most award-winning sport, which was Ultimate Frisbee, which only I sucked at. Then Ginger, first in the class, her headband worn like a crown over her broom of curls, Queen of Alabaster, that was Ginger. Then the others, and after that it was Deni and me, side by side, those aviators on her head, her brother's army jacket tied by the arms around her waist. Deni kept twisting on the steps, looking back, hunting out Eva, who was in the back of the pack, Shift beside her, neither of them talking, at least according to Deni, who was doing all the spying.

Into the sun we went, our ragtag O'Sixteen fourteen plus one.

The sky so blue. There was an American kestrel overhead. There was a trio of finches on the telephone line, already losing their luster, and right around Oyster Way, where we turned, we spied a lesser yellowleg, its wings brown and spotted like Bambi.

"Early proof of the start of migration season," Ms. Isabel said, parts of her words rippled back by the breeze. Early proof of migration starting too soon.

We all stopped. We duly noted. I glanced east, over one shoulder, past Chang and Taneisha, past Dascher and Becca, and there was Eva, her smile megawatt. Next I saw why: Shift. Hood up, madras shorts, and Eva's power binoculars pressed to his eyes. Those were Barbie-pink binoculars—pinker than Pepto. They were an Eva find at the St. Mark's White Elephant Sale; I had been there, and so had Deni, when Eva had negotiated. Eva took that pink prize wherever she went—to the beach, to the birds, to the lighthouse—and now, for that moment, she had given it up; she had placed it in the hands of Shift, a guy nobody knew.

"What's that about?" Deni said, because she'd turned, too.

"Guess she thinks he could use a little help with the birds."

"Eva, the naïve."

"Eva, the generous."

Eva, who saw things nobody could see, who chose *Vanishing Cities* as her Project Flow. All the hotels, the streets, the kitchen chairs, the bedrooms that lived invisibly—that had been swept away by winds or cracked by earthquakes or gobbled down. To Eva every inch of before was romantic history. Everything was submerged or on the verge of going under. Atlantis, for example, which Plato said was swallowed by the sea. Port Royal, Jamaica, which fell, in 1692, into its harbor after an earthquake rattled it around.

Five thousand people, Eva says. A city bigger than Boston. Gone. Disappeared. Just like Edingsville Beach, South Carolina, two centuries later—high rent and hoi polloi, a "playground for rich planters" (she read, from some book) that went down on both knees to a sweep of hurricanes. Shishmaref is disappearing, Eva would say, pointing to a place just below the Arctic Circle on a map. Venice will soon be gone. The Maldives. She'd lean close. She'd whisper the names. She'd sit back and close her eyes, and we'd watch the trance that she'd become, that she was. She was pretty on the outside. She was even prettier inside. She kept time and all its layers whole in the channels of her mind.

But back to Deni, who was giving me one of her stares beneath her spectacular eyebrows.

I stared back, shrugged, understood. Worrying was Deni's Job Number One. She'd lost the big things in life. A brother first (Afghanistan) and then a father (hole in the heart). The news that had changed Deni's life and consequently changed Deni had arrived in suits seven months apart, a knock on the door—the army people, the police— and who could blame her for the thoughts she had, the days she didn't trust, the plans she was forever putting into place, the precautions she took. *Shore Up.* That was Deni's Project Flow. Dams, dikes, levees, green-blue corridors, sea gates, surge control, blue dunes, oyster reefs, wrap the city of Manhattan up in plastic, float Venice on buoys.

Do something.

Mitigate the risks.

Do not disappear.

Deni was cautious on behalf of every one of us.

Deni was taking care.

"We'll keep an eye on her, okay?" I said.

"Smells like trouble," Deni said. "Her giving her find over to him."

"They're just binoculars."

"We're talking about Eva," she said. "And a guy who calls himself Shift."

Down Oyster Way. Toward the sanctuary. Across the crushed shells where the cars of summer parked. Toward the stubby bushes and the narrow boardwalk with the thick-rope rails and the sign: RESPECT. PRESERVE. That's where the sanctuary began. Ms. Isabel, up in front, was dialing the buttons on her lavender coat as she thought. She was lecturing about the stress on birds of changing climates, environmental heat, environmental endurance, and now she was turning the dahlia in her hair, as if she could somehow turn clocks back to a time when birds could fly wherever they wished—no factories, smokestacks, hot air, ozone blips. Keep walking. We did. There were swans in the pond that we passed—*our* swans, we said, of the family Anatidae, of the genus *Cygnus*— *Anatidae* and *Cygnus* being the kind of words that hold a thing in place, keep a swan from vanishing. There were red tips on the black birds in the trees. There was a tanager on a brambly branch and it opened its mouth to sing.

"Bird manners," Ms. Isabel said, and we took out our notebooks and our pens; we drew, as she had taught us to draw, the shape of the wings and the song. *If you look at the world, you will love the world*—that was Ms. Isabel's motto. *If you love the world, you will save it.*

We looked. We drew. We listened. We walked deeper in. Through the green shade, beneath the tree cover, into the smell of pine, old moss, cracked shells, root rot. In a soft clearing of pine needles, we stopped and formed a circle and for the first time that day Ms. Isabel actually looked at us. She stopped thinking about the birds. She started counting.

Twelve. Thirteen. Fourteen. Shift.

He was leaning against a giant oak—his hood up and Eva's binoculars still hanging from his neck by a cord. He had one knee bent and one flip-flop foot pressed against the tree bark. He was taller than the rest of us, and his eyes were so unreadable that he might have been wearing shades. There was moss furring up the branches above Shift's head, nests in the knot of some foothold, wings up high, deer in the shade. There was a breeze in the tops of the trees, two dragonflies with silver wings, the stirrings of a hawk.

"Shift," Shift said.

She took him in. Paused as if he were another foreign creature, a bird of paradise, a strange new species. "Shift," she said, and then she wrote it in the book she carried, and that was that. We stood in that circle on the pine-needle floor, the smell of salt and feathers and green so close. She took a yellow book out of her bag. She began to read. "'People change the world,'" she started, then flipped to another page. "'Faustian restlessness is one of the defining characteristics of humans,'" she read. She touched the dahlia in her hair and turned more pages, careful, squinting. She began again:

> "'The Neanderthals lived in Europe for more
> than a hundred thousand years and during
> that period they had no more impact on their
> surroundings than any other large vertebrate.
> There is every reason to believe that if humans
> had not arrived on the scene, the Neanderthals
> would be there still, along with the wild horses
> and the woolly rhinos. With the capacity to rep-
> resent the world in signs and symbols comes the
> capacity to change it, which, as it happens, is
> also the capacity to destroy it. A tiny set of genetic
> variations divides us from the Neanderthals,
> but that has made all the difference.'"

She stopped, looked up, caught our eyes, had our attention. "Elizabeth Kolbert," she said. *"The Sixth Extinction."*

She turned her head toward a rustling in the trees. We turned, too. It was there—the great blue heron with its bearded feathers, its yellow eyes, its strength: *Ardea hero-dias*. "Ruler of the earth, according to the Seminole tribe," Ms. Isabel said, leaving Elizabeth Kolbert for her birds. We watched the mighty creature crunch its neck, then stretch. It spread its rusty feathers. It shook its plume.

"The Bird will make sure that all things are put in their proper places on earth," somebody said.

Ms. Isabel turned.

"You know the Seminole legend, Shift?" she asked, because he was the one who'd said it.

"I guess."

"Somebody teach it to you?"

He shrugged.

"Hmmmm," she said, writing something in her book. "Hmmmm. Yes. Thank you, Shift. The heron," she now said, to the rest of us, "puts things into their places. According to legend. Just like Mr. Shift said."

Twelve, thirteen, fourteen.

Shift.

4.

Midmorning that day was Algebra 2: (xy)(n) =. It was Deni
with her stare on and Shift with Eva's binoculars, and Eva
looking possessive, rubbing her finger under her nose like
she does when she is dreaming or thinking or wishing. "I
can see all the way to Atlantis," she'd say, dreamily. "I can
see Last Island."

"Atlantis is gone," Deni would correct her, but Eva never
listened.

Focus on the math, I thought. Focus on the quiz. Focus
with the sky so bright above us.

$=$

$x(n)$
multiplied by $y(n)$
Math was symbols. I preferred words.

I sketched taxonomy charts in the margins of the
worksheet. I got called on for an answer, and I was wrong.
"You should do your best in everything," Mickey would
say when the report cards came in. "I am," I'd tell her, and

she couldn't prove me wrong. Nobody knows (for real, for true) how hard someone is trying.

Lunch was the sandwiches we'd brought from home on the picnic tables with the graffiti carved into the weathered wood: TANEISHA + TINY TINA. That was last year's news. ULTIMATE FRISBEE. That was forever. ITALIAN LOVE SONGS RULE. Which is what Mario sang, with his baritone voice; you couldn't believe the size of the voice that short kid had. There was graffiti from now and graffiti from years ago, rumors of graffiti from The Year of Our Birth. We couldn't prove it, but we thought, maybe. Maybe that Cupid. Maybe that arrow. Maybe that MARRY ME, PLEASE, BRUCE SPRINGSTEEN. Maybe that broken heart was from someone we knew. Maybe it belonged to our mothers.

"You watching this?" Deni, leaning over her chicken salad, said.

"On it," I said, looking up from my Tupperware applesauce, Mott's, not homemade; Mickey wasn't a homemade-sauce mother. And there was Eva, at table number three, her binoculars still on borrow.

"Not like he needs the binoculars to see the mayo on his wheat bread," Deni said. "I can see the mayo from here." If there was any condiment of which Deni vociferously disapproved, it was mayo. Shift was sinking fast.

"She looks happy."

"That girl has no defense system," Deni said. "She'd flunk a test on precautions."

"Guy knows something about herons," I said. "And Seminoles."

"Guy got lucky."

"Guy isn't half-bad-looking."

"Please. Can't even see his face, thanks to the hood."

The breeze blew in. It teased our wax paper, Ziplocs, paper bags, catching us in a scramble of chase and snatch. By the time we had collected our things, the bell had rung, and Mr. Friedley was out, sending us back into the school and up the spiral stairs and onto Level 3. To Pompeii and the city. To Trap the Metaphors, which involved, on that day (I remember this) cirrus clouds, rain in buckets, sun on the anchor of one shoulder.

We had Art after that—the sound of our charcoal sticks working in time to the tune the kindergartners were singing until Mr. Friedley came by and asked for silence. After that, it was 3 p.m. and the bell was ringing and the school day was finally done. We gathered at Alabaster's door. It was the hour of the Slurpee.

"Yo," Deni said to Eva, practically accosting her. "You coming to Rosie's?"

Which wasn't usually a question anybody ever asked, because Slurpees in off-season was our best-friend tradition. Slurpees was our gathering hour, our talk-it-over time, our gossip. Slurpees was unhitching our Modes from the racks at school, strapping our backpacks to our shoulders, and going.

But there was something about the way Eva was standing there, her ribbons of blond hair twining around her neck, her color high, her hands distracted, and Deni knew. She had her antennae way up, she was expecting as much, she was on the defense, standing close.

"Not so sure," Eva said.

"Not so *sure*?" Deni pressed.

"Think I'll skip it today."

"Something else to do?"

"Maybe?" Eva shrugged. She looked at Deni, looked at me, looked at her ten sparkle-decaled fingernails. "You have a Slurpee for me, okay?" Eva said to Deni, sweet as Eva always was, because Eva wasn't the kind of girl who would hurt on purpose. She was just the kind of girl who loved too much, stretched too thin, went way out of proportion too quickly, saw things that weren't there. The kind of girl who would loan her best find to a guy who'd kept his hood up all day.

We turned. There, on cue, was Shift. His flip-flops were a little sandy with the outdoor classes' wear and tear. He was standing among us, but mostly standing beside Eva, her binoculars dangling casual at his neck.

"Shift," Deni said.

"Yeah?" he answered.

"Shift. That's your name."

"Um. Yeah." His voice was a big shrug, like he'd been asked the question a thousand times before, like the uncoolest of uncool things would be to stand there and explain.

"You coming?" Deni finally asked me.

"I'm coming," I said.

I keyed on my roller skates. Deni revved up her Gem. We left Eva where she was, pink up high in her cheeks.

Shift.

First name?

Last name?

We had no clue.

We rolled, we glided to Rosie's. We had one Slurpee each, and then we split another, and then Mr. Carl, Alabaster's janitor, drove up in his 1962 Wrangler—top down, radio on. Rosie brought him a double cone of orange spice as if she operated a drive-in, but fact of the matter: Rosie was Mr. Carl's wife.

I caught the sound of the radio on his weather station. Some bunch of clouds forming way south and east. Clouds with the air of Africa in them, and the wetness of an ocean, and the height of a skyscraper, the reporter was saying, which was what the reporters on weather were always saying, nothing to write home about, something far away, and they were just words.

We'd been through every version of weather on Haven.

We knew water inside and out.

Some reporter on the radio couldn't scare us.

5.

Here I should probably explain the rules, the lines in the sand, the ins and outs of Haven. We were a people shaped by extremes. Too much and too little were in our genes.

To be specific:

Too little was the size of things—the dimension of our island, the we-fit-inside-it-bank-turned-school, the quality of restaurants, the quantity of bridges.

Too much was The Season—Memorial Day through Labor Day. Vacationeers by the boatload, bikinis by the square inch, coolers by the mile, a puke-able waft of SPFs. The longest lines at night were at Dippy's Icy Creams. The longest lines by day circled the lighthouse. During The Season the public trash bins were volcanic eruptions, the songbirds were scarce, the deer hid where you couldn't find them, the hamburgers were priced like mini filets mignons, and the rentable bikes streamed up, streamed down. At the Mini Amuse the Giant Wheel turned, the Alice in Wonderland teased, the dozen giraffes on the merry-go-round looked demoralized and beat. At Dusker's Five and Dime the hermit crabs in the painted shells sold for exorbitant fees.

Whoever was up there in the little planes that dragged the advertising banners around would have looked down and seen the flopped hats, crusted towels, tippy shovels, broken castles, and bands of Frisbee fliers—Vacationeers, each one. Whoever was up there looking down would not have seen the bona fides, the Year-Rounders, the us, because we weren't on the beach. We were too employed renting out the bikes, flipping the burgers, scooping the Dippy's, cranking up the carousel, veering the Vacationeers out of riptides—to get out and be *seen*. From the age of very young we had been taught to maximize The Season, which was code for keeping the minimum wage coming, which was another way of saying that we stepped out of the way, we subserved, for the three hot months of summer.

We Year-Rounders had been babies together, toddlers together, kindergartners together, Alabasterans. We had a pact: Let the infiltrators be and watch them leave and don't divide to conquer. We knew that what mattered most of all was us, and that we'd be there for us, and that we would not allow the outside world to actually dilute us. Like I said, we knew our water.

Six miles long. One-half mile wide.

Haven.

Go forth and conquer *together*.

6.

I woke to the sound of Old Carmen's transistor news. A ripple wind was kicking the sound waves my way. *Wind speeds,* someone was saying. *Updrafts. Eye.* Something was continent-size and massing, whirling and frisking, but that's what storms do. They collect themselves. They spin. They kick and moan and spit their way toward the minuscule Caribbean, scratch the stratosphere, and blow. Most storms don't make it all that far. Their chimneys pop. Their speeds collapse. They blow out to sea, disorganize.

I lay in my bed with the window open, listening to the radio words and the ocean. I lay there wondering if it was just another dream or a touch of déjà vu—this radio voice in my room, in my head, in the breeze. I pulled the thin paisley sheet off my legs and stared around at the room—the planked floor cool and the ceiling so low that when I stood I had to crouch, except in the room's middle, where the roof rose to a peak.

It was September. I was seventeen. The only Mira Banul in the miniature family of Banuls. Banul was my name and my species. In every school photo ever taken, I have the same expression: *What? Me?* I have the same Mickey-cuts-my-hair hair, the same spangle of freckles across my left cheekbone, the same unerasable lopsided stare. "You could try to smile," Mickey would say, but Jasper Lee, my perfect, brilliant brother, gave himself last-word status every time. "You do the Banuls proud," he'd say. And I'd look at him and feel so full of love that my heart would want to scream.

Jasper Lee—he never had a school pic taken. Not a single, stupid one.

Along the one edge of that attic sprawled the velvet couch—emerald in the sun, purple in the shadows, secure as a castle. In a bucket by its side were the snake, the frog, the turtle, and the walrus that I'd won during a good-luck streak at the Mini Amuse. Over there was the old walnut cupboard, just four feet high, where Mickey left the dishes my aunt had left behind. We never used them. We never sold them. We never talked about what had happened. *Not a story worth telling.* That's what Mickey had said. I'd moved into the attic when my brother came around, when he needed the second downstairs room as his own. I took it over, took it on, found room for me. The attic, its adjacent bathroom, the photographs that my aunt had left, too, the portrait of her in the frame. The best picture of my aunt is her at twenty-six years old, her long bangs disguising her eyes.

It said ME, 26, along the edge of the picture in ink.

Which is the only way I knew.

I stepped from the attic through the sliding door onto the deck. The tide was out, the edge of the sea against the horizon. The sun was a minor ridge of pink. Ginger's black lab was out in the sand, playing a game of Territory with a spotted mixed-breed I had never seen before, and there was Old Carmen, wrapped up in her blankets, on her swatch of sand. I closed my eyes, and the radio voice droned. Sahara something. Wind speeds 68. Caribbean crawl, no, not a crawl, a stall.

Haven was ready for anything. They'd pumped new sand onto our beaches the summer before—big pipes tossing out wet stuff from the ocean floor. They'd piled the dunes in front of the beachfront homes. They'd pieced new rocks together in black vertical juts. They'd said, *Be prepared for anything,* and we were. Our closets and basements and storage coves were rife with plywood and nails and duct tape. Our pantries were full of flashlights, batteries, cans, crackers, water jugs, candles, and the otherwise stuff that was stocked front and center in the hardware store that never closed.

Our training was impeccable.

We were used to weather. We were *proud* of being used to weather. Onto posts, signs, stucco, brick, inside our basements, we marked the places where the waters had, through the years, risen, like other people mark the growing inches of kids. In restaurants we hung photos of historic storms. In the DVDs they sold at the gasoline stations, they told the stories of our previous survivals.

But *this* storm.

This storm had stalled.

I pulled my hair into a ponytail. I watched the dogs chasing each other's tails. I saw Old Carmen stand and wobble down toward the sea. In the downstairs distance, in the paisley-plaid kitchen with the mustard-gold oven and fridge, I heard Mickey—her TV snapped off, her scrapple in the pan, because it was Wednesday, an Elaprase cocktail day, by which I mean a rumble-across-the-bridge-and-drive-another-hour-and-park-in-Visitors'-at-Memorial-Hospital day. They had a Jasper Lee bed on the second floor. They had a needle they hooked into his arm, a line that dripped, and a bunch of old magazines, but Mickey didn't read them. Mickey sat with Jasper Lee, talked to Jasper Lee, pulled puzzles, Monopoly, Crazy Eights, checkers from the canvas Bag of Tricks that they hauled hospital-way each week, and my brother always won.

Every Wednesday, this is how it was—cocktail day. Look up Elaprase, and they'll tell you this: It's a purified form of human iduronate-2-sulfatase, shown to improve "walking capacity," shown to reduce "spleen volume." Ask me, and I'll explain: It's the best shot we have at Jasper Lee not getting worse. The Elaprase does my brother's enzyming for him. It costs a lot. My mother drives. My brother sits. The government pays.

Which is the story of us, the Banuls, and if you loved a brother like I love my brother, you'd learn the hyphenated language, too. It'd be the only way you could ever think of to make that hard part of him part of you. To share it, somehow. To say, best as you could, "I am in this with you."

Wednesday. Mickey was making breakfast, and Jasper Lee was in his bed, lying there beneath the model planes that Deni and Eva and I had found as kits and brought home and assembled and glued and painted and hung from transparent strings thumbtacked to the ceiling. By his door were his wooden canes, which I'd painted in candy-cane colors. On his sill was his tin soldier army, which I'd found tossed in a can at the White Elephant. His special-size Velcro shoes for his special-size feet were, as always, beneath his bed. His curtains were closed, the curtains that Mickey had sewn from remnants she'd found—fabric cars, fabric adventures.

And there, on the bureau, nothing but sand. No mirror ("Be gone," Jasper Lee had said). No brush or comb ("You kidding me?"). No Haven paraphernalia ("I have some pride."). But sand, yes, film canisters of sand—eBayed out of its native habitats, sent by way of first-class mail, labeled with a chunky marker on masking tape. Jasper Lee had Corsica sand; Smith Mountain Lake sand; Cecina, Italy, sand. He had sand from the South China Sea and sand from Masaya, Nicaragua, and sand from the islands of Hawaii. He had canisters of chip, flint, spark from all over the world, and he had expertise—decipherings and decodings about the magic life of sand. Sand as interlocking crystals and three-armed sponge spicules. Sand as star shapes, heart shapes, tiny baby shells. Sand as micro sea urchin spines, rocking dodecahedra, precious garnets, feldspar, magnetite, quartz. Sand as fish bones, sand dollars, mica, forams, shipwreck dust, shark teeth, and broken dinner plates.

"Think about it," Jasper Lee said. "The more you knock around a grain of sand, the smoother and more polished it becomes. The heavier the wave, the more powerful the crystal. Trample it, pound it, toss it, scrape it, dig it, build it, crush it, but what have you done? You cannot defeat sand. Sand is victorious. Sand washes in, sand washes out, sand goes its own which-ing way."

Sand was what Jasper Lee knew. Sand was what Jasper Lee *owned*; it would have been my brother's Project Flow— Jasper Lee, who, in the early part of the sunny days, caned his way through the house and out the back door into the Zone, toward the gangplank Mickey had built to ease the path up and over the dunes. The gangplank we arranged after every storm and at the start of every year.

Captive coming, my little brother would say. *Captive on his way.* Stopping and standing at the top of the dune and looking out to the sea. Calling it high tide or low, even though Mickey and I already knew. The tides. The sand. The birds. The salt. He'd drag his body out there in the morning chill and find his place to be. He'd drop down beside his bucket, shovel in, watch the seagulls scatter and return, the little pipers. He'd say, *Don't run off*, and sometimes I wouldn't, and he'd pull his fingers through the sand, let that sand shimmer down to earth. His thick fingers. Those sandy grains. The lock and interlock of my brother, weather, time.

We'll build a castle, he'd look up and say to me. *We'll fortify.*

My brother had plans. He had plans and sand vocabulary. The best castles ever built were the ones that he designed. The best sand ever caught was the sand that he curated. The best soul on the planet was him. I might have been medium at most everything, but I had arrogance all over me about my brother, Jasper Lee. He was the best brother ever, and today was cocktail day, which was also scrapple day, though I was a sunny-side-up girl myself.

"Hey," I said, when I came downstairs, dressed for school and for the sun.

"Morning," Mickey said.

She had her apron on, her faded jeans with the ripped hems, her painted T-shirt and tie-dyed flip-flops. Her hair had been thickened by the scrapple steam, and there was heat behind her freckles. She was tall and skinny, long dark hair with blunt-chopped ends and little ribbons of gray near her face. Mickey's shoulder blades were her most memorable part. No matter what she wore or how she stood, those two back wings angled out. They were where and how she stored her strength, which she needed plenty of; everywhere you looked there was proof of that. The basket of unpaid bills by the silver breadbox. The Post-it notes on the refrigerator. The calendar that she'd thumbtacked to the kitchen wall— Jasper Lee's doctor appointments, Jasper Lee's therapy sessions, all the Mickey gigs that Mickey did to try to keep our family's engines purring. Mondays and Fridays: Front Desk at the Gray Lady Nursing Home. Tuesdays and Thursdays: kiln duty at the pottery shop. Saturday afternoons: care for the O'Sullivan triplets. Sunday afternoons: some seamstress work, if she could get it. Mickey searched, snagged, took what she could. She marked it down on the calendar. She stuck the dates to the wall.

"Can I convince you?" she asked that day, meaning the scrapple beneath the steam. She was the kind of pretty the people who knew her saw best. Jeans shaggy, cuticles torn, hair just hanging, a few odd strands of gray—maybe that's how other people saw Mickey. But that's not how we saw her, Jasper Lee and me. We saw everything Mickey did for us, and all the ways she loved, which included Wednesday-morning scrapple, which is also called *pon haus*, which has been defined, by the Wiki, no less, as little more than mush. Food taxonomy.

"Not a snowball's chance," I said, yanking out my own frying pan and plopping it down. I took two eggs from the carton. I turned on my fire. I swiped a pad of butter. I sunny-sided, taking my place beside my mother. We kept our backs to the turned-off TV.

"Finish the scrapple and I'll get him up?"

"Finish my eggs," I said, "and I'll get him."

I gave her my spatula, my flame, my perfect yolks. I left her like that—manning two pans, and two fires. There was no storm in our sky. Only blue. Only light. Only the smell of all the salt in the sea.

7.

I would wish not. That's what my little brother always said, his Wednesday mantra. "I would wish not. Please."

He would say it lying there on his bed, in the crack of light. He'd say it as I pulled his curtains wide, those fabric cars running a wavy north and south. I'd open his window, let in the breeze. I'd get his clothes out of the dresser drawer, toss them his way. I'd sit on the corner of his mattress, low to the floor, especially arranged, and nudge him on the arm.

"Hey."

"I would wish not," he'd say.

"Please?"

I'd sit on the edge of his bed as he squeezed his gray eyes shut, so many versions of wishing. I'd watch him and see everything he struggled with—walking a straight line, pedaling a bike, digging a sand castle, balancing a spoon, keeping his tongue inside his mouth, staying unangry even if his hands were a little bit like claws and his face kept flattening. *Mickey, someone ironed my face.* I'd sit there and try to see an ounce of Mickey in him, and then I'd try to imagine his dad, which was not the same as trying to imagine my own—different people and no photograph that I'd ever found of either. I'd never asked Mickey which one of her children's fathers she'd loved the best, or *if* she'd loved them, even, because what kind of question is that, and how would it not make her sad, and did I even want the answer?

My dad had been a deserter; that's all Mickey had said. Jasper Lee's dad had been one of those, too, gone after the pregnancy news and too lily-livered to ever show up here and say, *Hello and how are you, and how is our son, you need something, Mickey?* I never met any man I could call Dad. But in the morning, when my brother wished not, I tried to see a father in my brother's bones, in the genes he'd left, in the enzyme he'd been robbed of. I tried to see a dad, but all I could see was a kid who wished not for a machine and a hospital bed, a kid who would give anything at all to be medium smart, medium blond, medium fine, school pic after ordinary school pic.

Medical history of my brother in a nutshell: Adenoids removed to help him sleep. Bilevel positive airway pressure machine—BiPAP—to help him breathe. Spine permanently curved because his fragile bones prevented a fix. Hernias removed, and then more hernias.

If you need a reason not to complain about your so-called problems—the B on your Algebra 2, the tear in the seam of your jeans, the bruise above your heart, the overkill worry of your one best friend and the incredible naïveté of the other, the fact that Mario never notices you, that he sings baritone past you, that he's short and he never looks up—then I invite you to imagine my brother. On Wednesdays he wished not, and would you not, too? Wished not to rise, not to be driven, not to be hooked up, not to be cocktailed. In our house by the beach on the island of Haven, Wednesdays were Wish Not. We practiced the religion of persuasion.

"Come on, little brother."

Groan.

"Open your eyes."

He opened his eyes.

"I'm skipping today for tomorrow."

"Tomorrow will be here in no time."

"Maybe for you."

"Maybe for you, too. Someday."

"Maybe," he said. "Yeah."

The breeze through the window took his planes for a spin—the barnstormer, the Fokker, the Sopwith Camel. They went one way and then snapped back, and I thought of the day that Deni and Eva and I had hung them there, Jasper Lee lying on the bed beneath us while we cut the nylon string with our teeth. "Works of art," Eva had said.

She had twisted her hair into a dozen braids. She had stood there, on my brother's bed, craning her neck, looking up. Then she'd stepped off the bed and lay flat on the wide-planked floor. "Your planes," she'd said. "They fly eternal. No storm will ever reach them, no quake will ever fold them, no continental shelf will ever take them down, they will live on and on. Eternal," she'd said again. She said it in that small but lovely voice she had. She said it with emotion. She said it as if suddenly she could see the future, too, and not just stratospheres of once. Deni and I stood on the trembling mattress. Jasper Lee lay there flat. We heard her voice. It echoed like prayer. I looked down and my little brother was crying.

Eternal. What a word it was, to a boy who might not live to be adult.

"Come on," I said again that Wednesday. Nudging him, picking his clothes up from one side of the bed and placing them closer to where he could reach them.

He lay there. I sat there. We felt the breeze, both of us; heard the sound of someone talking on Old Carmen's radio.

"She wearing her boots?" Jasper Lee finally asked, closing his eyes again.

"Guess so."

"She fishing?"

I turned, strained, looked out the window.

"She's getting started. You hear that?" I said.

"What?"

"Mickey's making your scrapple."

"Scrapple is gross."

"I know."

"You've got to tell her."

"Tell her what?"

"That I'm not a fan of scrapple."

Every Wednesday I made the promise. Every Wednesday I broke it. I knew what Jasper Lee knew—that Mickey needed the scrapple more than Jasper Lee wanted scrapple. I knew what I couldn't fix—that she needed to believe she could do something more for her second child than what the doctors and the Elaprase offered.

Jasper Lee would always be crooked. He would always be fragile. He would never be graceful. His tongue would always be too big for his mouth. Jasper Lee would always be the person people could not see first, because people see what they want to see, at least in a quick and judging first glance. Mickey hated this about people. Mickey hated it for her son. She made him scrapple because making scrapple was active, it was one of the ways that Mickey loved him out loud.

"Just go with it, all right? Get up?"

"I'm getting up. Can't you see me getting up?"

He pulled the sheet away with the best of his two hands. Then he turned in his bed.

8.

There's no traffic to speak of off-season at Haven. There's hardly
any traffic on the bridge. But there's mainland traffic on the
way to Memorial, and Mickey did her best to beat it. That
day Mickey had taken her apron off and combed her hair.
Jasper Lee had caned his way down the hall, out the door,
over the pebbles, to the car. I'd waved goodbye and gone
inside, up the steps, into my room, when my cell phone
rang, and it was Deni.

"She's at it again," she said, no hello, no stop. "I was
walking Cinnamon Nose, right? By the beach, right? And
there were Eva and Shift out on the rocks." I thought of
Deni and her Bernese mountain dog, prettiest dog I'd ever
seen. Dog had a good leash yank in him. Cinnamon Nose
made spying tough on Deni, but she was keen on practicing
the art.

"Which rocks?"

"South end."

"What time?"

"Early."

I was putting my bracelets on, my eleven earrings. I was slipping the key around my neck, touching the bruise it left. I was pulling the ponytail higher on my head and checking the mirror and feeling the breeze through the window. I was listening but I was distracted, too—remembering the look on Jasper Lee's face when Mickey had backed her Mini Cooper down the pebble drive. His eyes were everlasting gray. The cherry-red Cooper with the dragging back fender was headed off toward the bridge—Mickey's hand held high and Jasper Lee's hand held low, waving their opposite goodbyes.

"Mira?" I heard Deni now. "You listening?"

"I'm listening."

"You sound like you're miles and miles away."

"How could I be miles and miles away?" I asked. "In Haven?"

"Don't you care what happens to Eva?"

"Of course I care what happens to Eva. But she hasn't been kidnapped, Deni. She's met someone new. This is what Eva *does*."

"I don't have a good feeling."

"Do you ever?"

"He came out of nowhere. He only has one name. Who shows up in Haven to go to Alabaster, middle of September?"

"A transfer," I said. "I guess."

"Eva's already in, whole hog."

"Don't go crazy on her, Deni."

"I'm not crazy. I'm just careful."

Of course, Deni wasn't completely wrong. Eva was an overtruster. She'd bring every ball of furry-stray home. She'd set up lemonade stands for the feeble. She'd think that she could cure the brokenhearted with her triple-flavored taffy. Eva was a bleeding heart and her heart was bigger than two Grand Canyons. Loving Eva was keeping an eye on her. It came with the package.

Deni needed needing most of all. We loved her in spite of herself.

That morning, Deni kept talking until she stopped. I mean: She kept talking and I went down into the kitchen to start cleaning up, water running, pan scrubbing while Deni talked and I uh-huh'd in the pauses, and then we said goodbye. I'd left my backpack upstairs and so I hurried up to get it—past the paintings on the striped stair wall and past the clay pots that sat one pot per step, each with a face that Mickey had carved at Sandy Sacks, the community art center where she worked. She'd made the pieces in the off hours when the bisque was cooling in the kiln. She'd brought each home, and she'd laughed at them, and we'd tried to guess who she'd been thinking of when she carved the nose, the brow, the grin. *Not telling*, she'd say. *Secrets are secrets*. She used oxides instead of glazes to give the creatures color. Their teeth were gray. Their eyes were hollow.

We called them gargoyles behind her back and then in front of her, but she wouldn't give in, wouldn't tell her secrets.

Just people I knew, she'd say. *Acquaintances.*

In my room, the breeze was moving the curtains around, the paisley bedspread, the skirts in the closet. I rolled the sliding door open, brought my cactus inside, placed it on the bureau beside the photo of my aunt. Then I went back out onto the deck and took one last look around for dolphins, noticed the waves coming in at an angle, no Old Carmen. I'd have been late for school if I stood up there any longer. I'd be getting a call from Deni first, and then a reminder from Mr. Friedley. So I stepped back inside. I bolted the door. I grabbed the backpack and my skates and headed down the stairs.

At the landing I heard a sound in my brother's room. There was something stirring the model planes—the breeze through the shingles and plaster. I stood for a moment and watched the planes fly. I thought of Jasper Lee, wishing not. I thought of Mickey behind the wheel of the car, the hair she combed getting tangled at once because she liked her window down.

I didn't see the forgotten Bag of Tricks until I was halfway gone. It'd be a long day at Memorial, I thought.

And felt a sudden wash of sorry.

9.

Too late for homeroom. Too late, even with my skates keyed to my Skechers and my backpack aerodynamically strapped and no sandwich in the Ziploc; the morning had run out of time. I was Bonnie Blair, crunched at the waist. I rollered north toward the sanctuary, took some air over the curb, pumped until I was up to steady speed, and the breeze was strong, it was working with me. At the broken shells of the parking lot, I stopped, unkeyed my skates, then ran, quiet as I could over the wide white crunch.

I heard the birds before I heard the O'Sixteens, some of their songs close and some of them falling in from the faraway coves. I followed the clattering bridge, passed the pond and the sleeping swans, and now the breeze was in the tops of the trees, and I was still on the path, edging the empty culs-de-sac of trees and nests, until there they were, in the shade, campfire style.

Ms. Isabel's lavender coat was dragging behind her. Mario was up on his backpack for the purpose of height.

Chang held her azalea-pink blade like a dish, and Tiny Tina and Taneisha were holding hands, no secrets to those two, not since a year before, when Tiny Tina had stood up on the lunch-table bench and announced that she was in love and Taneisha was hers: "Taneisha Green, you are off the market. O-fish-o-lee."

I didn't see Deni at first, then there she was, sitting against a cypress whose lower branches were long gone, the stubs of them like the start of deer horns. She had her arms crossed over the tied sleeves of her brother's jacket. She had her tic-tac-toe T-shirt on and her khaki shorts and a pair of hiking boots, scuffed at the reinforced toes. Her eyes were disappointed, cautious. They looked from me and then to them and then back again.

Where the hell have you been? her eyes said.

I need some help here.

Look.

I looked to where she was looking. I saw: Eva and Shift sharing the stump of a tree. They were sitting back to back, propped against each other, sideways to the rest of us, like they had known each other all their lives, like they were *O-fish-o-lee*. There was moss hanging like Mardi Gras beads above their heads. There was a blackbird in their tree. Shift's hood was up. The binoculars were back around Eva's neck, but on Shift's denim lap was a perfect conch shell, still sweating with the salts of the sea. Shells were an Eva specialty. She found

47

them, whole and unbroken. She gave the best as gifts, her name written inside with a gold glitter pen, as if she were the shell's creator.

What do you want me to do about it? my eyes said back.

Something?

What *something?*

She gave him a shell, Mira. A shell.

"Mira Banul," Ms. Isabel said. "Please take a seat."

There was a pine-needle clearing between Marco and Dascher, and I chose that. Slipped the backpack off. Set down the skates. I took out my notebook and I glanced back at Deni and she was staring into the middle distance, only half listening to Ms. Isabel telling the story Ms. Isabel wished she didn't have to tell. About the rising sea levels and the habitat loss, about invasive species, vegetation shifts, birds getting all messed up in the head—confused on the subjects of migration and breeding, nesting and care. Birds showing up at the wrong time in the wrong places, Ms. Isabel was saying, her roller cart at her feet, her coat full of fluff, her buttons wound loose on their threads.

"Look up," Ms. Isabel said. "Listen. Love."

Eva lifted her eyes toward the tops of the trees.

Deni took a long, painful look at me.

We sat quiet.

There was the *whooo* of an owl.

"I don't know how I could love much more," Eva said, the kind of thing she was unafraid to say to an entire audience of O'Sixteens. The kind of thing they let her say, without bothering to tease.

"That's the tragedy of it, isn't it," Ms. Isabel said. And then she looked at Shift and dialed the dahlia in her dreads.

I waited, I kept waiting, for Shift to look up, to look back. Tell me who you are, Shift.

It was time to stand and find our way back, through the gates, to the white-crunch parking lot.

The atmosphere zinged with blue.

There were no clouds to speak of.

There was a wind, and on the wind were the birds that had followed us out, and, with the wind, Ginger's gold hair ruffled and the hem of Ms. Isabel's lavender coat never touched the ground.

Deni caught up with me. We walked, not talking, my skates hanging from their tied laces between us.

"Whole world's falling apart," Deni finally said. Which is what Deni said both times she got her news, both times she lost big and forever. *Whole world's falling apart.* It wasn't one hundred percent true. It wasn't one hundred percent false. I managed the skates out of the way. Put my arm around her.

Ahead of us, out in front, Eva and Shift were leading the O'Sixteens back toward Main and the reconstituted

bank, toward Mr. Friedley and the songs of the kindergartners, the unrelenting sorrows of John Steinbeck. They were
a solid half block ahead—not touching, not talking, then
talking and not talking again. Eva's long blond hair was
tangled with ringlets and wind—a thick, yellow fog. She
had her pink Skechers on and her orange short-shorts and a
white, gauzy shirt with long sleeves; her skin was still pearly
brown from the summer sun. Shift was wearing cropped
jeans and the same sweatshirt, the same thin-at-the-heels
flip-flops. His hood had flown back and his hair was wild—
lighter than you'd expect on a guy that dark. He had a good
foot of height on Eva. He carried his hands inside his pockets. He squeezed his thin spiral-bound between his right
arm and his chest. He took one step to every two of Eva's.
He had his shoulders hulked up, to his ears.

I watched them, I studied them, I turned to watch Ms.
Isabel, who was watching them, too, and I remembered Eva
two weeks before, top of the world. We'd ridden our Modes
half the skinny length of Haven, rolling and cruising down
the centerline of Main—*Woo-hoo, the invaders are gone.*
We'd stopped where the island had stopped, the northern-
most tip, the lighthouse, those red and white stripes, like
old barbershop stripes, like the colors I'd painted Jasper
Lee's canes.

It was Deni, Eva, and me. It was one day before school
was to start. We climbed the empty belly of the lighthouse
and went out by the rails and caught our breath and stood

there looking. The myriad sea was that way. The whole wet world of hidden things—octopi and killer whales, blue crustaceans, redfins, walleyes, purple snails, sunken treasure, mermaids. A couple of bright sailboats were skimming the ocean's top. A couple of far-off freighters were chugging. You could see China if you squinted hard enough, even if China could never see us, but Eva—Eva could see everything: She could see the submerged city of Alexandria and its Pharos lighthouse. She could see Port Royal and the fallen thousands. She could see the big hotel on Last Island, underwater, and the billiard parlor of Edingsville Beach, South Carolina. She could see Diamond City and Thompson's Beach and all the other places the sea had swallowed. She could see her history best from way up there. She pointed, and we listened. She named the lost places, and I remember thinking about how big her heart was, how much she could love, how she should be mayor someday.

"Eva," Deni called now. "Wait up a sec."

But her words got tied up with the wind.

11.

Dr. Edwards had a beard. He had a mustache, he had side-burns, he had hair that flopped across his brow and down into his eyes. He was gray all over except for a thatch near his right ear. He favored that thatch. Touched it when he talked, and when we listened.

We'd made it past Algebra to History.

Down the hall, under Ms. Isabel's orchestration, the O'Seventeens were reciting the periodic table—beryllium, magnesium, calcium, strontium, barium, radium, then back up to scandium. In Dr. Edwards's room, we were still in Pompeii with the first century and the Romans, what he called a resorter's paradise. Homes for the wealthy in Pompeii, he was saying. Brothels for the bored. Paved streets, tourist traffic, slaves for hire, open squares—Dr. Edwards was drawing us the picture, throwing images up on the screen, quizzing us on what we had promised to read the night before. That hot lump of rock called Mount Vesuvius.

The spout of pumice and gas. The shower of ash. The air thickened like soup and the buildings falling down and the people trapped by the pyroclastic surge. One hundred miles per hour of poison rushing down—poison gas and murderous rock and ash. The pyroclastic surge of Pompeii swallowed everything at once. It suffocated the stay-behinds. Knocked them flat where they had stood.

Two thousand dead, Dr. Edwards said.

"I believed that I was perishing with the world, and the world with me," Shift, of all people, said. Shift of the Quotes, I was beginning to see. Shift of the timely memory. I could see Deni thinking one word: *Pah-leeeze*. I could see Eva thinking, *Shift of my dreams*. I could see some trouble coming, but the thing is, I didn't foresee the trouble that came.

"Pliny the Younger," Dr. Edwards attributed, with a nod.

"Yeah."

"And your name again, sir?"

"Shift."

"Thank you, Mr. Shift. You are precisely right. Pliny believed the world was perishing. He lived to say it wasn't."

Shift covered more of his head with the hood. Eva looked at Deni, who looked at me. They were chanting nickel, palladium, platinum, darmstadtium down the hall, Ms. Isabel singing the lead. They were going all out on "Frère

Jacques" two floors down. Mr. Friedley was seconds away from sounding the bell.

"An historian among us," Dr. Edwards said.

Shift. The first new student at Alabaster in ten years had been crowned "historian," a word none of the rest of us had earned.

Eva's smile said it all.

The wind had started to turn.

12.

There was no Mini Cooper on the pebble pad when I got home. Nothing. Traffic on the bridge, I thought.

Eva, Deni, and I had each gone our separate Mode way—Deni rumbling the Gem, and me riding my wheels, and Eva pedaling her board, Shift beside her. He had that thin notebook of his still clenched under his arm. His legs were long; he didn't have to run. We went north and south and east, two of us alone.

On the couch by the bay window I threw my backpack down beside Mickey's apron, Mickey's secondhand purses, Mickey's collection of sun hats. I grabbed a jar of Mickey's granola mix, ran up the steps and rolled open the door to the deck. The sea was getting its gnarly face on, looking a little dented and chipped. There was a bank of gray clouds in the distance and Old Carmen on the rocks, her radio volumed up. News. *Eye of the storm headed out to sea. Worst of the storm hurtling east, hurtling past.*

The Ultimates were rambling in—cutting over the dunes, kicking off their shoes, running the quickest line toward the sea froth. Chang dumped her backpack on the high sand, snatched her blade, flicked it, and it flew—a straight up-and-back boomerang whip. Taneisha raised her arm and snatched it, easy, nothing to it. She flicked it right back out, aiming for a trick, but the blade slammed against a breeze and fell into the sea.

I could hear Taneisha's bracelets ringing. I could see her cupping her hands around her mouth and calling to Mario, who was running, plunging into the cool temps of the sea, laughing inside the soak of it, his long hair hanging down like the ears of a sheepdog. He snapped up the Frisbee and high-kicked his way back to shore, his jeans hanging low below his waist.

It was just some breeze. It was just that gray patch of clouds—way out there near China—and now the team had its game going again, its after-school practice of flicks and cuts, corkscrews and bombs, bookend maneuvers. Chang had a whistle around her neck, team-captain style. Mario was reckless with his art. Taneisha was off with her toss. Every time she missed, Tiny Tina called out, "Love you!"

It took a while before they saw me, before Ginger, her plum-colored sundress filling up like a balloon, then deflating, according to the theatrics of the breeze, pointed at me, up on the deck, said, "Hey. Yo. Mira. You're in."

The blade went short from Chang to Mario to Taneisha and then it took off and the breeze had it, the breeze rinsing it free, swiping it high and hinged, the sound of Taneisha's gold bracelets still ringing. I stood by the rail of that deck. I raised my hand to the sky. I stopped the bullet speed. The Ultimates hollered high fives at me.

Mira Banul. Blade in hand. Medium nothing, right then.

The breeze blowing the wrong way, I bent at the knees, angled my wrist, and webbed my fingers across the disk and let go. It swished. Over the rail, into the sky, across the dune, where it caught a whirlpool of air and spun and Chang began to run, her long legs chipping across the wet sand, her black hair tossing forward, like a hat fallen down on her head. The blade was a kite on a string. It wobbled, then fell. Bounced on the sand, then rolled the wrong way, and now all of the Ultimates were running, dragging their game farther on, away, throwing a goodbye wave over their shoulders. Chang and Mario out in front, their long black hair snapping. Ginger in the middle. Taneisha and Tiny Tina in the back, holding hands as they ran, Tiny Tina an entire head and some shoulders over the girl she loved. The bright blade shone like a beacon. Atlantic City stood in the distance, its neon lights muted by the afternoon sun.

I wished Mickey and Jasper Lee would come home, wondered vaguely what they were up to, when Deni would call, what Eva knew about Shift and when she would tell us. The tide was going to turn. Old Carmen was watching the sea. She stood up, hitched her waders to her waist with her hands in her pockets, then walked down to the tide and went in up to her knees, didn't flinch. She stood there, staring, for the longest time, then reached in and rinsed both hands in the salt of the sea. There was a dolphin way out there, or maybe two. There were gulls collecting like clouds and swooping low, screaming some nonsense. The waves were full of extra froth and vigor.

I didn't find Mickey's message until later.

Call me, sweetie. Soon.

13.

One blue Slurpee. Two blue Slurpees. Three blue Slurpees. Four. Counting the way I'd learned to count in First Aid and Rescue—Rosie's sister being the paramedic instructor and always influenced by flavors.

The phone rang through.

I punched END, tried again, nothing.

Third time I dialed, it rang five and a half rings, and then I got the echo noise of Memorial, the beep of some machine, the slipping squeak of rubber soles, until finally, after that, the alto version of my mother's voice—not a good sign, not what I wanted to hear. Low alto was Mickey controlling her breaths and monitoring her tone. It was Mickey trying to protect me from something.

"Mickey?" I said, leaving the deck for my attic, too little pacing room.

My back to the breeze. My phone to one ear, my free hand cupping the other. I had to hear everything she said. The first time. No repeating.

"Tell me," I said.

Nothing.

"Please?"

There were all kinds of Memorial noises now. Wheel *vroom* on linoleum. Background shuffle. The *flip flop* of Mickey's shoes, because she was on the move, looking for a quieter wedge of hospital hall; I'd seen that hall, I'd hop-scotched that hall, I knew the shine of its every painted-like-everything's-fine green inch. Seven blue Slurpees. Eight blue slurpees. Nine.

"Mickey?"

"It's Jasper Lee."

If I talked, she couldn't, so I said nothing. If I pressed, she'd just have to pause again, breathe in steady and breathe out steady, keep her voice slow, low. Ten blue Slurpees. Eleven.

"He's had a reaction, Mira."

I stopped walking my tight circle. Turned to face the breeze that was blowing in through the open sliding door. On the beach, the Ultimates had returned, were running north after each other, toward the longest arm of rocks. There was a grayer patch of sky. Old Carmen stood with one hand over her eyes, salute style. That tide rising, higher.

"Anaphylaxis. Angioedema. Tachypnea. Dysphonia," Mickey was saying, and a gull, maybe a couple of gulls screamed, and I couldn't hear the in-between words, couldn't hear the next part, stepped out of my room, into the hall.

The bathroom door was rattling on its hinges. A bottle of shampoo had blown off the ledge into the claw-foot tub.

"It was like—we were done," Mickey was saying. "It was like any other infusion day—the needle out, the gauze on, packing to go. You know? We were by the elevator. We were pressing DOWN—he was, Jasper Lee—and the next thing I knew his face was bright red, and he was wheezing, saying, 'I can't see,' and then he said, 'Everything tastes like metal, tastes like I swallowed the Mini Cooper keys, did I swallow the keys?' and thank God, Mira, thank God I was standing right there, because he slumped, but he didn't hit the floor, he'd have hit his head if he'd hit the floor, because I had him, at least I had him, right? And he was in my arms and I ran him back to the machines, to the bed, to Vidushi—you remember Vidushi? The nurse? She saw me coming."

I could picture her there, in the fake happy of bright hospital lights. I could put her into place in my freaked imagination—the chipped blue polish of her toenails like bruises on the beat-up pads of her flip-flops, that long slash-tear in the hem of her jeans. I could see Mickey, but I couldn't see Jasper Lee. Not where he was, not who he was with, not what was happening to the bravest guy I knew.

"Is he—?"

"Intubated," Mickey said. "And . . ." She swallowed, stopped, didn't start again, as if she couldn't remember, had forgotten where I was, that I was me, alone, in the hand-me-down house behind the dunes beside the shore, Old Carmen acting weird out there, the Ultimates gone again. "Isotonic crystalloid," Mickey said. "Isotonic crystalloid, because they said he needed fluids. Fluids and air. That's what they said. Oh. Sweetie," she gasped. She must have put her hand over her mouth, covering up whatever her voice was doing then, but I could hear her trying to right herself, trying to turn the voice channel back to low alto, the delivery channel, so that she could be Mickey, a mom with two kids. Mickey, a mom who had to get this right.

"I think he'll be all right," she started again. "I think—"

But she stopped right there, didn't think out loud, and now I was pacing again, back in the attic bedroom where everything went slanty—the stuffed animals and the good china and the low ceiling. In the world outside, the waves were coming in, higher than Old Carmen's knees, close and getting closer. Everyone I loved most was on the other side of the sea, across a bridge, in a hospital that was painted all-wrong green, and I couldn't save them; I was medium everything, helpless. My crooked, enzyme-leaching, too-short handsome brother had a tube in his throat and crystal something in his veins and he thought that he had swallowed car keys. I was two hours from where I needed to be. I was two hours and stranded. Useless.

Be brave. That's what Jasper Lee would want me to do.

"The doctors know what they're doing," I said. Finally.

"Of course," Mickey said.

"And Jasper Lee's a fighter."

"Always."

"A reaction, Mickey. Not a condition. Right? Beatable?"

"I don't know everything," she said. "Not yet."

And even though I'm the world's original hater of not knowing, even though I didn't know the hyphenates yet, the terms for this emergency, even though I was crying, but crying so that Mickey couldn't hear me, I said, straight as I could, sister to Home of the Brave, "You tell Jasper Lee that when he gets home, we'll build him a new plane."

"I will."

"And that it will fly eternal."

"Okay."

"You tell him his Bag of Tricks is here waiting. And that I'll make him the eggs and I'll eat the scrapple, but he has to come home."

"We'll be here overnight," Mickey said. "At the very least."

"I know."

"We'll be here, but I'll be checking in, all right? Stay near your phone? Keep it charged?" She was getting her voice back, her feet beneath her, she was standing up straighter, I could tell. "I love you." That's what Mickey said to me. And then the line went dead.

14.

Maybe you think I had options. Hitching a ride. Calling a taxi. Getting a police escort off the island, over the bridge, to Memorial. Maybe you think I should have done something, acted, used my big vocabulary for something actually useful. But Deni's mom was at work. Eva was somewhere with Shift. Ms. Isabel was back in the bird sanctuary, where rule number one was to keep the electronics off, and all Mr. Friedley drove was a beat-up Harley, no room for two, and you know what a taxi would cost from Haven to Memorial? A taxi would cost all Mickey's jobs put together, and then some.

Jasper Lee would be all right because he had to be all right, that's what I thought. Mickey needed me manning the house. Fixing it pretty so that when she drove home with Jasper Lee just fine up front, she'd have nothing to do but ooh and ahhh at the cleanliness of it all, the immaculate order—*Oh, Mira, you thought of everything.* She'd sit down with her toasted English muffin and its melted peanut butter, watch the heat rise off the tea, tell me the story and how it all, in the end, okayed out. There was dried yolk on the red plate in the scratched basin of the sink. I cleaned it. There were pillows and hats needing straightening. I hung coats. I hooked hats. I carried old purses to the closet.

First rule when you feel afraid is to act. A lesson from Deni.

I cleaned the hell out of that house.

I don't know why I figured the windows needed cleaning, too, the inside of the range, the handle of the refrigerator, the empty places in the pantry. I dusted the porcelain figurines. I rinsed the saltwater taffy bowl. I took a swipe at the ceramic ladies on the steps. I Lysoled down the toilets. The shampoo that had fallen into the claw-foot tub upstairs had left a little stain of goo; there was no more goo by the time I finished. I had never, in my entire life, cleaned a house so well. I had never counted so many minutes. An hour went by. Two. Deni didn't call, Eva didn't, either, and I didn't hear from Mickey, didn't get the call she was supposed to make to say Jasper Lee was fine, it was a silly false alarm. *Hey, Mira,* Mickey was supposed to call and say. *We're coming home. We're one hour short of the bridge.*

I worked until every surface was buffed and straightened and the kitchen smelled like lemons and bleach. I slid down the hall, out the front door, to the pebble lawn, my heart set on the sight of the Mini Cooper. Nothing. Then I turned and looked back at the house—its stilty legs, its isosceles hat, its cedar shingles the color of cracked earth, its shutters a tint called Pumpkin Spice, its oddball mailbox, its front-door wreath built out of bright canaries, made special at the How to Live store.

This was it, our place, no more mortgage due, thanks to Mickey's hard work, thanks to her priorities: *Own where you live.* This was it, thanks to my aunt, who had left it and Mickey behind.

"We need some help here," I said to the breeze, to the grayer sky. "*He* does. My brother. Jasper Lee." I sent the words up to a passing gull. I looked down at my phone. I begged it. *Ring.* But in my freckled hand the phone was silent, and Haven was off-season still, and the gull had stopped to rest on a telephone pole, clicking its head from side to side, no opinion, yet, no text.

Maybe fifteen minutes went by, maybe thirty. Maybe only seconds. But I know for sure that at some point next I heard a strange little knocking. Speed of a jump rope. Quality of a thud.

Harder, then softer.

Near-seeming.

Far.

Something knocking.

I went back into the house and out the back door into the Zone.

Thud thud u dud thud.

It wasn't loud. But it was there.

15.

In the Zone was all the junk we never used but hadn't tossed away. The old bikes, deflated rafts, shovels, and horseshoes. The junk we never used but had never bothered dumping. It was all there, and so was the sound:

Thud u dud u dud thud thud.

Not coming from the crease in the chairs, not coming from the ropes of the rafts, not coming from the bright blue bucket that Jasper Lee used to wear on his head when he stomped by the sea, before we knew the name of the thing that he had. Not coming from the cooler and not coming from the phone in my hand, I kept checking the phone in my hand, I kept thinking Mickey would call me soon. *Call me.*

But I was closer now, the sound was harder now, the sound was coming from the dark beneath the house— coming, it finally seemed to me, from a row of cinder blocks, where, years ago, Mickey had parked a wrinkled pleather trunk, that trunk like a queen upon a throne. My dress-up wings were in there. My sequins as jewels. My hairband tiaras. My ruby shoes. "There for when you'll need it," Mickey had said, like it was dowry material, worth a little something, but it was only one more bump of junk in the shade, and I'd not thought of it for years, but now, yes, I was headed that way, toward the trunk, and when I stopped and bent close, I saw: The trunk's latch had popped.

The noise grew more frantic, as if it could sense me near. It changed its velocity, telegraphic. A mouse, I speculated, had chewed its way in. Or maybe a pair of bunnies had been tricked in, a magician's gift. Something was in there and it needed to get out. I touched the key above my heart. Gave it a rub for good luck.

I took one quick breath, and I took another quick breath.

I flipped up the top of that trunk.

She was a true-silver silver with pale blue eyes, a pure white single sock, a triangle of pink for a nose, whiskers the color of a web. No name, no bell, no collar dangled from her neck. You couldn't call her a newborn. But she wasn't a fully grown cat. She was trapped inside a wing. She had a string of beads around her neck. She had been trying, it was clear, to dig her trapped way out.

She mewed. She was frantic. Her tail was a crazy SOS.

"Hey, hey, hey," I said, reaching in and pulling her free. "Hey. You. It's okay."

I held her to my chest. She was anxious against my heart. I flipped the lid back down and we sat like that on the trunk beneath the house on the safe side of the dunes.

"I've got a brother," I told that cat. "Wait till you meet him."

16.

Deni was there in a Gem flash. Flying through the front door, out the back, finding me in the Zone with the kitten on my lap, my butt on the lid of that trunk.

"Sterling," I told her.

"Huh?"

"Sterling. That's the name of the cat."

Deni plopped down beside me. Stuck out her hand. Got herself a whisker tickle, a pink-tongued lick, a meow. "Inside *there*?" she said, pointing to the trunk with her chin, continuing the conversation we'd had on the phone, seemed like just seconds ago, Deni was that fast, Gem and all. Deni had listened—about the stray, about my brother.

I shrugged now. Clueless.

"But how'd she get in?"

"Someone must have tipped the lid," I said. "And then she climbed in and the wind shut it down. I guess. Cat in a trap."

"And you heard her crying?"

"I heard a bunch of tail whacking. That's what I heard."

"Christ," Deni said. "Something new every day."

I loosened my grip on the cat. She padded my belly like my belly was a pillow, didn't run away, settled down. Like nothing had happened, like it was all usual, just some everyday business to wind up in a trunk that hadn't been opened for years. The cat began to wash herself, her tail waving like a flag. It was a performance, a good one. It left us in silence, Deni and me and the Zone. Then Sterling stood on all fours and padded my belly and sang out with a full cat's meow.

"Got a pair of lungs on her," Deni said.

"Yeah."

"You keeping her?"

"Only just found her."

"You think she likes Friskies?" Deni reached into her canvas purse, size of a Hefty bag. She'd made it herself in Art two years before—hand-stitched the seams, sewed some decals on, reinforced its stitches. She was famous for it. Now she was digging in and pulling out a brand-name bag, ripping it along its stitching line. "'Tantalizing mix of ocean fish, salmon, tuna, shrimp, and crab flavors, plus a touch of seaweed,'" she said, mimicking the ad. "'For seafood lovin' cats.'"

She pulled a fistful of the bits into her hand. Turned her hand into a tray, palm up. Sterling sniffed and chewed and decided. Friskies it was.

"You didn't have to do that," I said.

"It was on my way. I got a discount, thanks to all my purchases for dear old Cinnamon Nose."

"Yeah. Still. Appreciate it."

I leaned against Deni, watched Sterling feast. I thought about all the times I'd wished Deni would worry less, ease up on her endless contemplating, her caution signs, her armorizing the world she knew. She sat there beside me, feeding that cat, guarding our Zone, not talking Eva, not talking Shift.

"You know my dad?" is what she finally said, and of course, one hundred percent, I had. Known him for all my years up until a few years ago, when he was killed by the empty place in his heart.

"Yeah."

"He would have loved this story of your cat. Every creature, every thing, like Dad always said, is a candidate for saving."

I pictured the barrel of Deni's dad, the gray stubble and the silver buzz cut, the collar he wore on Sundays to preach at St. Mark's Episcopal, the White Elephant sale he conducted in the church basement three times a year. Deni's dad had been a preacher man. He'd been the original advocate for salvage.

There was light in the spikes of Deni's hair. There was the day reflected in the mirror of her aviators. There was a piece of string tied around her ankle and the Afghanistan campaign anodized medal she'd triple-knotted onto that string, in everlasting honor of her brother. The sleeves of his army jacket were tied at her waist. Her chin was on her hand like a Rodin thinker.

"I have a good feeling about your brother," she said then. "I have a feeling he'll be just fine; he'll be home soon."

"That's what I told Mickey."

"Mickey's going to be all right, too."

"I know."

"She's going to love what you've done with the house," Deni said, and she tried to laugh, so I did, too.

17.

The sky was curtained with clouds by the time Deni went home.
Gray purple and amber purple, with a violet purple farther
out. The birds were flying closer still and the tide was
high and feisty, the foam shearing loose from the sea and
bouncing down the shoreline. The dune planks rattled
when the breeze kicked in. The window boxes beneath the
front bay window complained. The monsters of the sea
were out there churning—the strange and lovelies, the dolphins I could see, the see-through fantasia, the Christmas
tree worm, the *Marrus orthocanna*, which the textbooks call
a rocket, which looks like a cross between a jellyfish and
a sea anemone.

Sterling and I had a whisker contract; she could stay
as long as she understood that her business would get done
in the big Tupperware I'd filled with sand and left on the
floor of the upstairs bathroom.

We'd talked.

She was a smart kitten with the brains of a cat.

Respectful.

Tomorrow, I promised myself, I'd find out where Sterling really lived. I'd put up some posters. Make the roller-skating rounds. Inquire. But it was late, and I'd had enough ache for one day. That cat was good company. She roped between my legs as I cooked up a second pair of eggs. She drank her cold milk first. She relished her Friskies.

Mickey called once. She called again. She said Jasper Lee was stable but the doctors needed time. A night or two, maybe three, probably more. Jasper Lee wants to say hi, he can't actually say hi, but he is saying hi with his hand right now, waving to you.

I raised my hand. Waved back. Said nothing about Sterling. Nothing about the wind kicking up and the birds flying low, because on TV the weather people were saying that a giant storm way out at sea had stalled—one thousand cloud miles caught on a jet stream and carried away, out of reach. The storm chimney was popping, the storm system was squalling, the storm was sliding around and losing its head. The gray and purple clouds were the edge of something dying. The wind was incidental.

"Get some sleep," Mickey said.

"Yeah."

"Lock the doors."

"I will."

"You need anything, call Deni's mom."

"I'll call Deni," I said. "Deni's enough."

I could feel Mickey smiling through the phone.

"Say hi to Jasper Lee," I said.

"Okay, we're saying good night," she said.

18.

Right now, telling you this, I remember four years ago. I am thirteen and Jasper Lee is six, and it is November. A steel-plate sky. A nude-tone beach. Dune grasses tall, scrawny, wheat-colored. The surfers are out by Cedars, catching the year's tallest risers. The diner is open, the hardware store, Malarky's Pub, Uncle Willy's Pancakes, the bank, Rosie's, the Roman Catholic, the Come as You Are, the St. Mark's Episcopal, Deni's dad still upright and in charge. The traffic lights on off-season blink.

"We should do it," Eva says.

"Do what?" Deni takes the tease; she asks. We are at my house, back in the Zone. We're playing horseshoe toss with the stakes planted into the uptilt of the dunes. Deni is winning, Jasper Lee is keeping score, Eva is bored.

"End to end," she says. "Main Street. Winner takes all."

I cross the Zone, finagle the latch, dig into the trunk for the old dress-up things and grab the finest pair of wings—3-D and glitter, more ladybug than angel, bird, or fairy. "If we're doing it, we'll need some of this," I say. There's a red-and-blue towel with wide stripes tossed over the picket fence, and I snatch that, too, and now the game is on, they understand—Eva unplanting the pair of Fourth of July pennants from the white-weave basket of my mother's bike and Deni running into the house and up the stairs and coming back down with that stuffed turtle I won at the Mini Amuse in her hands. "Mascot," she says, her glasses pushed up even then onto the top of her head.

We should do it. End to end.

Rite of passage, on Haven.

My house is at Mid. We'll start back at South, finish at North. These are the rules we give to ourselves. We single-file out of the Zone, in through the house, out onto the street. I've got Jasper Lee on piggyback and my skates by their laces around my neck. Deni stuffs the turtle onto the Gem's dashboard and pushes from behind. Eva carries her Taperkick board like a baby. We push, we roll, we carry four blocks west and ten blocks south, to Haven's farthest tip, where Atlantic City in the distance is every casino color inside a veil of gray.

Jasper Lee will go with Team Gem—a group decision. I knot the striped towel at his neck, lower him down into the passenger's seat, make sure his cape is fly-ready through the golf cart's open back end. Deni adjusts her turtle mascot: front-and-dashboard-center. Eva sticks the two pennant flags into her braids so that they flap like elephant ears on either side of her head, and now I've got my wings tied on, and we are ready, three across plus one, wheels drawn up to an imaginary line. End to end. Six miles, no sprint. Haven is as flat as God ever made a place. Our topographic troubles will be potholes and sand slides and all the roughened places on four-lane Main, where we will keep to the gold divider lines of the perfect center, Year-Rounder traffic beware.

"To the lighthouse," Eva shouts. "Ready! Set! Now!" A turn of a key, a bend in the knees, a push, and we fly. Eva whooping and the Gem purring and my skates counting a steady *one-two one-two* glide, and you should see the cape on my super brother fly. Speed-skater style I crouch, adjust my wings, catch a ripple of November breeze, and maybe I'm medium good at most things, but I'm extra-large good at this. I'm crazy happy swift. The skates beneath me fly. The key bangs a bigger bruise above my heart. Eva, meanwhile, rides her Taperkick straight as a pin, her big pennants flapping like Dumbo ears. The Gem is all easy gleam, and Jasper Lee's super cape is flying and Deni's hands are on the wheel.

Six miles end to end, and the day is gray, but we are color, and the traffic is light, and it is yielding, and we are riding the divider lines, south to north, rite of passage. And when a car shows up it honks us on. And when a bike goes by, it rings its bell, and when Chang and Mario and some of the other O'Sixteens show up, casual at first, they run the golden center line behind us, yelping how it'll be their turn next, how they could beat us any day, you should have told us today's the day, until they tire of the chase, and Mr. Porter from Uncle Willy's comes out and stands on the sidewalk and salutes, like we are the parade, like he can remember, still, because he can remember, still, the day he went end to end, on his own.

The world runs different when you ride it through on wheels. The world runs medium blur, wet-paint style: Haven does. Houses on flamingo legs, houses spilled on pebble lawns, houses with their motorboats up front, like dogs on leashes, and then the swatches of retail, the red and orange of the CLOSED UNTIL NEXT SUMMER signs, the high top hat of Rosie's, the plastic flowers in the barrels by the diner. The big orange Godzilla legs of the water tank. The Alice in Wonderland characters of the Mini Amuse. My ladybug wings are flapping flapping flapping. Eva is riding straight as a pin. Deni is talking mascot talk to the stuffed turtle, and the smile on my kid brother's face is ear to ear, it's everything, it's rite of passage now. His cape flying. His happy soaring. His difference invisible now, and to hell with iduronate-2-sulfatase enzyme, I remember thinking, to hell with recycling mucopolysaccharides, to hell with the name of the disease, to hell with taxonomy, there's no right name for everything that's wrong, don't put a number on

Jasper Lee, don't put a percentage chance, just give him a wide-striped towel with a little shine and call it what it is: a super brother's superpower.

It was a gray day. It was November. The sun was waiting at the northern tip, behind the barbershop stripe of the lighthouse. Six miles is a lot of miles when all you've got is Modes and a center line. Six miles is lungs burning, feet blistering, one toenail turning blue, we never figure out why. Six miles is talking and whooping and smiling at first, and then it's a pretty kind of silence above the *whirr* of wheels. Six miles is winner take all, and we were winners, we took all.

We were hand in hand at the northern tip.

We were winners, four across the line, super cape and super mascot, ears and wings end-to-end flying. We were us. We were before.

19.

In the early evening of the day that Jasper Lee couldn't come home, I cooked myself more eggs sunny-side up, like I said. I poured milk into one of Mickey's glitter-glazed bowls and Friskies into the palm of my hand, and Sterling feasted. I left the dirty dishes in the sink because everything else was incredibly clean, and tomorrow would be another day.

We were supposed to have another day.

You know those sound machines that pretend to be waterfalls, log fires, whales? Right then the air outside sounded like machine rain on volume low. Like slosh, like slide, like someone shaking a sleeve full of beads. I climbed the stairs. I whistled *two three four* and Sterling came—her narrow body snaking between my calves, her whiskers like sugar that's been heated, pulled, and chilled. She said nothing on the stairs and nothing in my arms when I carried her from my room through the open door into the wet dusk. Beyond the balcony there were no stars, no moon, just rain.

The tide was halfway back and retreating. Far away, a yellow crack of lightning split the sky. The edge of that storm, I thought, blowing out to sea. I pictured it a hundred thousand feet high and a thousand miles wide and a storm eye the size of an island and pretty as a cathedral, because that's what Ms. Isabel had said, years ago—the eye of a storm is like a cathedral. She read it to us; I remember: "It has been likened to a cathedral with sacred carvings on the walls, stately balconies protruding, even pipe organs reaching to the clear, blue dome above."

Sacred carvings. Balconies. Pipe organs. The storm in retreat, putting on its show for the great whales and the ancient sharks and the hidden reefs, the vampire squid, the blob sculpins, the red-lipped batfish with its eyes like two domes. I thought of all those forecasters with their fancy weather machines, their computer models, their barometric reads, their promise: the storm headed the way of oblivion. They were, I'm telling you, sure.

No danger here.

No danger there.

Not the night I'm speaking of.

Sterling squirmed in my arms, tucked her head beneath my chin, kept herself out of the way of the rain. I thought of Jasper Lee and Mickey in the fake happy colors of Memorial, a line between them and the storm. Maybe Mickey was asleep in the visitors' chair. Maybe Jasper Lee was sleeping, too, the hospital gown with the blue snowflakes loose around his throat where the tube dug in. Or maybe the second patient bed in the double was empty, so Mickey was sleeping there, the curtain between the two beds drawn open and Mickey's flip-flops on the floor. Her knees would be tucked up, her body curved like a French Ç. Beep of the monitoring machines. Bar of light beneath the door, storm at her back.

There was the cool prickle of the rain in my hair, the tide going out, the soft flop of fish out in the watery sea. The wind curled and thickened and the birds flew low and dusk seemed loud to me. Sterling's tail was going *tick tick tick*, and her ears were cutting into the underbelly of my chin and her whiskers were quivery and now something *changed*, something went wrong inside the wind, until Sterling herself was pushing against me, from me, her silver fur turning to muscle. I thought for sure that she was going to fly—out of my arms, over the deck, into the dunes, into the evening, her tail ticking. That she was going back to wherever she'd come from, and already I was sorry, holding her tighter, telling her don't go, then telling her, promising, that I'd find her true owner tomorrow.

That's when I heard them: footsteps in the sand. Footsteps coming from the other side of the blockading fence, then onto the invisible part of the beach, then cutting the corner and heading for the gangplank—our gangplank, the one with the ropy rails that bridged over the dune that kept our house safe from sea treachery.

It was only dusk, but I could not see. We were not alone.

My phone in my pocket and Sterling in my arms, my mind roulette-wheeled through the choices I had, the possibilities. Deni with more Friskies, but she'd have called. Eva with news of a lost city found or a boy named Shift, but she was a front-door friend. Old Carmen, but that was stupid, because Old Carmen kept her distance, Old Carmen came and went and bothered nobody; there was nothing I could imagine Old Carmen needing. And then I thought maybe Mickey and Jasper Lee had come home, but I only thought it because I wanted it, there was no chance of that; I froze. Nobody I could imagine was coming for me. But somebody was down there, under the deck, in the Zone.

"Lock the doors," Mickey had said, but in Haven, off-season, we hardly did. *Lock the doors*, but now it was too late, too wet out there, and if I creaked just a little bit on that deck, if I moved, whatever had come would come for me. "Shhhh," I told Sterling. "Shhhh." The sound of feet on the gangplank going up, and then heading back down, and now the squeak of the shoes in the wet sand, and the sound of the rain in the breeze.

If I'd heard the back door open, I'd have 911'd. If I'd heard footfalls on the steps by the ceramic ladies, I'd have screamed. If I'd turned to find someone in the room behind me, I'd have bundled Sterling and taken a flying leap off the deck and into the dunes.

Nobody out there to hear me.

But that's not what happened. What happened is the footsteps stayed inside the Zone. What happened was a bumping and bending and rattling of things, a banging and sliding, a knocking of buckets against lids and tops against bottoms. Beneath the deck where I stood, someone was hunting, noisy and careless.

Ready.

Set.

Now.

Be still.

I held Sterling tight. I never touched my phone.

I never heard the back door open or the stairs creak. I only heard, after too much time, the gangplank groaning again, the stranger leaving.

It was early dark by then. I strained but all I could see was the hunch of a figure lit up by a brand-new lightning strike. A figure fast receding.

20.

I locked the doors. I closed the windows. I watted out the cottage—turned on every bulb, every spectrum of bright. The rain was falling harder now and Sterling was mewing and I said *shhh,* and poured her a fresh bowl of milk. I dug into the Friskies, put my hand out like a tray. She went from the milk to my hand, from my hand to the milk, and I complimented her on her bravery, told her wait till she meets Jasper Lee, a real trailblazer in the courage department.

"Doesn't even flinch," I said, about how Jasper Lee would sit on that hospital bed and open out his arm and take the needle with the enzymes. "Doesn't flinch at the start and doesn't flinch at the end when they take the needle out, swab off the blood, lay down a Band-Aid. He stands up like a grown man. Shakes the nurse's hand. Says goodbye and thank you, politest person you ever saw. They love him at Memorial, and you'll see why, Sterling. You'll see why. You'll love him, too."

That's what I said.

From the milk to my hand, from my hand to the milk, Sterling's ears were upright and her whiskers were drippy; that cat was a world-class listener. A curious cat, her tail going back and forth, and now I was telling her about Christmas on the island, the lights we string from place to place, the candles in the jars that Jasper Lee lights. Next I was saying about Halloween and the parade we do down on the beach, Jasper Lee in whatever costume Mickey and he make, piggyback riding place to place: *I don't want to scare anybody.* And after that maybe it was a story I told about how Deni and Eva and I had built those model planes that soared above my brother's room. Landing gear up, I told Sterling. Thrust reversers retracted. The combat aircraft painted to look like weather had already done it in. I told Sterling how Deni had done most of the gluing and Eva most of the painting and how we all three had strung each plane up, standing on Jasper Lee's bed while he sat below, praising our craft skills and engineering. "You sure know your mechanics," he'd said, and Eva, a straight C-minus in every Ms. Isabel class, almost died laughing before she caught her breath and said how a girl could get a big head if she stayed near my brother too long. It was shortly after that when Eva lay down on the floor and declared the planes eternal. I was thinking of this then, got her image in my head—her blond hair, her tip-of-a-turnip nose, her deliberate way of looking at things so she would not miss a detail. Everything to be lived or imagined. That was Eva. She didn't care one whit for terms.

I told Sterling about the little tin men and the road-trip curtains and the canisters of sand from all over the world—the island's best collection. I told her how Jasper Lee was interviewed for the local weekly, *The Sand Dollar*—the topic being his expertise in the crush that spills up from the sea. I told her how when the photographer came to take Jasper Lee's pic, he'd said there'd be no pic without my mother and me, because if he was going to be famous, *we* were going to be famous, didn't matter what we knew or didn't know about sand, only mattered that we were family, all for one. The united Banuls.

"Nine years old, and that's what he's saying," I was reciting to Sterling, who was licking my empty palm with her tongue, then licking herself clean under the shine of every light on. The rain was steady by now, and the winds were stronger than before, but they weren't howling, I didn't think they would be howling. They'd be gone by tomorrow. That fact was promised.

I stood. I checked for a view through the front bay window and the kitchen side window and the windows in the back. But all I could see by now was me. The windows like mirrors, a million reflections of medium and more-than-medium scared. Whatever had gone down in the Zone I'd discover the next day in the sun. We'd faced much worse, but even so, I had a crawly feeling inside.

Every five minutes I checked my phone. No Mickey. No Deni. No Eva. "Come on," I finally told Sterling, leaving every light on and grabbing the cat's Tupperware litter box and carrying it up the stairs. I slid it next to the claw-foot tub, and the cat purred. Her body swam between my calves, her tail a mop against my bones. There was a trace of warm milk on her whiskers.

"Time for bed, Sterling," I said, and she looked up at me, like she knew the drill, like she had nowhere else to go. I used the bathroom, took a shower, came back, and we were clean and ready as we'd be for many days now, but I had no idea what we'd gotten ready for.

The biggest prize I ever won at the Mini Amuse was a walrus, stuffed with foam. I dug it out from the couch and named it hers, arranged it nice on my bed. I made sure that cat understood; she was a real smart cat. She put a claim to it at once. Padded it down, curled her body up, licked her front paws, settled her chin.

"'Night, Sterling," I said, putting my *Wind in the Willows* T-shirt on and checking the sliding door lock once again and cutting the one bulb in my room. I stood looking out for a while, watching the inscrutable dark. The white teeth on the black sea seemed closer than before. Old Carmen had abandoned her post, gone to wherever she went when she wasn't at home by the sea.

The wind seemed harder, but there was nothing I could do. Tomorrow I would wake to find the sun. Tomorrow Mickey would call and Deni would ask, *You keeping that cat? Holding tight? Need me for something?* And I'd say, *Yeah. Yeah. No, I'm good.* Then Deni would tell me the morning news on Eva.

"'Night," I said again to Sterling.

One hand on that cat's head.

One on the tusk of that walrus.

21.

Later they would call it Monster, Colossal, Extreme. They would say twelve hundred miles wide and shattering. One hundred sixty miles per hour and gusting. An eye like a country of cathedrals. Power slurped straight from the sea. Broke the models, broke the measures, broke the rules.

Winner take all.

Sometimes sleep is easy; it takes you sly. Sometimes it runs ahead, leaves you wakeful, tricked in, memories instead of dreams. That night, in my mind, Mickey was home—her long hair in a loose knot, her toenails painted Memorial fake, her hands too small for the cup she was sipping from, the scent of fruit tea rising. That night, Jasper Lee was home, too, of course he was. He was tall, he was fine, he wasn't sick, he'd never been sick, he was sitting by the front door on a wooden stool, waiting on a canister of Cambodian sand. That night, Eva was lighting candlewicks inside mason jars and planting them on every sill, flowers growing like gardens above her ears, and she was saying, "Nope, girl, that must have been a dream. No thief in the Zone, Mira. The world is sweet." That night, end of that night, there came Deni, climbing the stairs and breathless in the attic, with a haul of Friskies on her back, Santa Claus–style.

"Just in case," she was saying.

Just in case.

Deni. You call her. She'll be there.

She wasn't there.

It was after midnight, and the rain was blowing hard. It was dark, and Sterling and I were sleeping and maybe dreaming, and you might have thought a locomotive was coming, you might have thought there'd be the big Evacuate Now—the horns that said, *Get yourselves out of here.* But it was late, and we believed what we had been told. That this storm was but a passing thing.

The only thing certain is the past, and even the past is up for grabs—both the textbook variety and the personal kind, and every single one of Eva's lost cities. I'm telling what I am telling, but I have to take it slow. It was dark, and it was night, and it came—a high-tide ride, four stories tall. I checked the records for that; that is the number. A high-tide surge that rose and rose and crashed against the lighthouse stripes, the anchored tankers, the sailboat sweets, the black boulders, the piers and the pebbles and the gutters of the houses by the edges of the sea, the laminated windows, the bridge between us and the world, and all the nests of all the birds in Ms. Isabel's sanctuary and the beard of the great blue heron. A colossal wave was coming, then it came: water tonnage. A mind-of-its-own monster, beating every single odd.

The big wave coming, the big wave crashing—up against the barriers and through the rocks and into the safe parts of the Zone. A wall of sound and then it was back again, closer, harder, at our door, knocking with its frothy fist.

And Sterling stood.

And Sterling growled.

And the lights ticked off downstairs.

And I was more afraid than I'd ever been.

I shot up from the bed. I yanked on my jeans and my Day-Glo waders, my khaki trench coat with the big buttons and the sash belt and the eight never-ending gonzo pockets. I stood, sick inside and off my balance, and listened, and yes: The wind was a beast. The rain was a horizontal slash, it was bullets up against the glass, it was the end of all things. I felt my way across the room, toward the closet. I fell to my knees. I couldn't swallow, could barely breathe, could hardly think, but then my hands were thinking for me— tossing aside the heaps of left-behind things until I finally found the trunk Mickey had prepared just in case "the big one" came, and yes, this was the big one. The big one did come. Out there, beyond me, the ocean was throwing a fit and sucking back. It was rushing forward, it was pissed-off hungry, it was full of rush and gush. I heard it, I could imagine it. It wasn't a dream.

Beneath the wads of old dresses and scarves and use-less things, beneath everything my aunt hadn't wanted and my mom hadn't tossed was the kit; I found it, blind, with my hands, dragged it out into the room, opened the lid. Extra water, fish in cans, chips in bags, peaches in sugar syrup, a mother lode of Hershey's Kisses, wrenches, toilet paper, matches, bug spray, candles, all those extra sets of batteries, and plastic sheets and plastic ponchos and the flashlight we called the doublewide.

I switched it on, and I could see.

It was too late for almost everything. Too late to plywood the windows. Too late to call for help. Too late to get out.

Think, Mira. Think. I counted Slurpees. I categorized. I put the moment into taxonomic order: Animalia, Chordata, Mammalia, Primates, Hominidae, *Homo, Homo sapiens*. Me. I may have been part of something so much bigger than myself, but it all came down to me.

The only defense against the storm would be the hurricane shutters my aunt had left us with—the solitary, rusted pair that ran across the sliding glass door to the deck. I turned the broad yellow eye of the doublewide in that direction. I stood and I walked—one step, another step: Mira Banul, be brave. I reached the shutters, lay the flash-light down, and cranked those things like my life depended on it, because it did. Sterling wound like a silver thread between my legs. "Home of the brave, home of the brave, home of the brave," I said, and the sound of the rain on the roof and on the walls was so gigantic, the sound of the winds and the surf so much bigger than before, that every time I said "home of the brave" to Sterling, I couldn't hear a single word I said.

"We're going to be all right," I yelled, but when I looked down at that cat threading between my legs, beneath the khaki hem of that coat, it looked like she was crying— her mouth wide open, her nose a perfect triangle, her tongue bubble-gum pink. And even though she had the mind and soul of a cat, she was the size of a kitten, and she was frightened. "Hey," I said, and I picked her up, and I kissed her nose, and I stuffed her into one of the eight never-ending pockets, and that's where Sterling stayed, not really a kitten, not actually a cat—nice and put, her head like a periscope, watching.

I could hear the waves out there, the waves and their teeth. I could hear the wind in the Zone, churning like a greased turnstile, picking things up and throwing things down, to hell with that thief—that was history. The stuff that happened next was up to me. The stuff that would go wrong would go wrong because I was out of a fix, or short on smarts, or too medium. I finished cranking. Sterling was pocket-tucked. My bare feet were hot in my knee-high wad-ers, and the next thing was next. Go downstairs, Mira. Go careful. Go slow. Breathe.

"Mira," I said out loud. "You are in charge."

In the kitchen the sink shivered with the plates I'd left undone, and with the smell of all those lemons, that bleach. The table was standing, the place mats arranged to serve three, the potato growing out its long tail in the tall, scrubbed glass practically glowed, effervescent. The notes we'd magneted to the refrigerator door had ripples in them, lifts and flaps, from the breeze that had made its way in, because now, even in the dark, I could see that there was a breeze in the room—in the tablecloth, in the curtains, in the dish towels, in the wall calendar where Mickey wrote our lives down. The breeze was in the room—in the folds, in the future.

Not a breeze.

A wind.

Coming, I guessed, from Jasper Lee's room, so that's where we went, Sterling and me and the boots and the coat and the doublewide—leaving the kitchen for the hall, nudging the door open with my foot, finding more gust than breeze blowing through the long band of Jasper Lee's windows which had, I guessed, been raised up by the pressure of the storm. I slammed each window shut. I locked each window tight. I caught an image of a girl in the reflective glass—of a girl and the head of a cat in the pocket of a trench coat, silver as a spoon. The girl's hair was plastered and her eyes were big.

The girl was me.

Above my head, the airplanes were dashing back and forth on their strings. On the floor by the door the Bag of Tricks was the loneliest thing I'd ever seen, and the soldiers on the windowsill had nothing on the storm, and the sand, all that prized-possession sand, the Jasper Lee collection—we couldn't lose that sand. I couldn't let my little brother down. I had to save what had so far saved him. That's when I decided, when I figured out my plan. When everything that happened next began.

"We're saving everything," I told that cat. "We're saving everything we can."

Categories upon categories of things.

Bermuda sunset sand. Vietnam War sand. Sand off the shore of Lake Placid. Sand dug out of Haven on a birthday and sand sent in from Australia and sand that was red and black and mystery sand and sand my brother had labeled THIS STUFF'S PURE GOLD. I slid each canister into the pockets of that trench coat, like rolls of coins, like ammunition, then I followed the light of the doublewide through the kitchen and up the stairs and into the attic room, where I unloaded, hiding the Jasper Lee collection in my sock drawer, among the fishnets my aunt had left behind.

Back downstairs, I swept the army of tin soldiers into the coat pockets, then hurried back upstairs and jangled them in with a drawer full of sweaters. Next on the rescue was the Bag of Tricks. After that: the decorated canes. Later: the *Nat Geo* magazines and that box where Jasper Lee kept what he wouldn't throw away, also both pairs of shoes that Mickey had paid extra for and the cruising shorts that my brother liked best.

I had a plan.

The plan saved me.

Without the plan I would have gone one hundred percent batshit crazy.

Up I went. Down. Until finally I had what I could get for Jasper Lee and it was Mickey's turn—the battery light thrown down across the square of her room, where I hardly ever went when she wasn't home. It was worse than sad in the bright, striped light. I sat, shivery and shaky, on the edge of Mickey's bed. Ran my hands across the thin, pale quilt, a patchwork, a gift, some lost story. Winter or summer, spring or fall, Mickey's bed had the patchwork on. It was a save I had to make, at least it was something.

Mickey kept her jewelry on her bureau in seashell dishes—bangles, hoops, and macramés. I swept them into my pockets. She kept her useful barrettes beside her favorite barrettes on a little wooden tree; I couldn't remember which was which and so they all went—into another pocket. She had a plastic box of porcelain tiles where she had tested her favorite oxide rubs, and I knew what they meant to her, how she studied them, how this would have mattered, so I took them.

I saved what I could. What I loved, what they loved, what I needed, what would be missed. I had my hands, I had my arms, I had my shoulders, I had eight pockets and a flashlight and I had to do something, because if I did nothing, I'd have died right there and then, I would have sunk down into a dark corner and cried tears bigger than any sea.

The twelve-hundred-mile-wide storm was near and coming nearer, over the heads and through the souls of all my pretty monsters.

I don't know when the dune was breached. I don't know when the gangplank buckled and crumpled and fell.

I don't know when the tongue of the sea reached the edge of the Zone or when the winds stirred the water there and drowned the sandy bikes, the woven chairs, the horseshoe rings, the pleather trunk, the half refrigerator, the bright blue bucket Jasper Lee wore on his head, king of the tidal parade. I don't know when the first trickle of water made its way into the house or when the trickle became a flood became what it ultimately was.

I just know that I was running out of time, and that I had something else I had to do, something we'd discussed a million times—at home, at First Aid and Rescue. Switch the natural gas to OFF. Go out in the roaring rain with a safety-kit wrench and count the valves—first up from the bottom. You turn it ninety degrees: off. You never ever turn it back on. You do this or you could find yourself in a red-hot blaze in the middle of a flood.

"You stay put," I told Sterling, pulling her from the pocket, laying her down on the walrus, telling her that every piece of everything in that room was hers to watch, by which I meant guard, through which I emphasized: *Don't let me down*, by which I also meant: I already miss you; I'm terrified; I'm doing what I can; please try to trust me. Her eyes were like sea glass. Her tail was wild as a flag.

I left her there, behind the shield of the hurricane shutters.

My heart crashed against my ribs.

22.

The wind was velocity, the rain was muscle, the wave and the wave after that surged up over the beach, over the dunes, past the pole legs of the first line of houses, through and across and back. Again and again. Farther. Spasms of speed.

I wrestled the front door until it seemed to break from its frame and the wind tore me out onto the porch. I huddled low. I took the slam of the storm and the sea. The seafoam was up inside my boots and the gas line was this skinny line beneath the big bay window. I fought the winds, took the porch steps down, one at a time, sliding and fighting. On the pebble lawn, the water was up to my knees, and I curled as I walked, I dragged my coat in through the thick foam and the debris I couldn't see until I was close enough to find the valve that was first from the ground. I found it. I fished around with the jaw of my wrench and I turned and I turned until I had the valve switched to a final OFF.

Don't ask me how.

Don't ask me about the houses where the valves stayed on.

Just this: They sparked blue and purple first, and then they smoked for days.

I remember nothing after that, except for taking a Mary Poppins wind so hard that it cracked my feet behind me, flapped my trench coat like a baby bird cruising tropical seas. Maybe it was the porch rail that saved me, my arms around it in a padlock. Maybe it was the wind dying back, maybe it was one of my *Delphinus* dolphins, one of my lovely monster friends, but I don't know, and then I saw it coming—a stop sign torn loose from its corner post and trapped in the wind. Edge over edge, red over silver, it hurtled with the wind, the doublewide catching its slice of speed like an old-time movie reel.

Who was going to hear me?

I remember, and then I don't remember after that. My thoughts were broken, and then my thoughts went black, and then the world went on without me.

23.

I came to in a pool of rain, a sprawl of knees and elbows on drowning porch boards. I opened my eyes to the sight of the flashlight scraping the storm with yellow line. I thought that the world was broken and what was the point and where were my mother and my brother and my two best friends? Where were they? How were they? Was this living or was this being dead, and then I remembered the things I'd saved: Sand with the socks. Soldiers with the sweaters. Bangles with the underwear. Mickey's quilt folded. Safe. Dry.

Maybe I'd made a mess, I'd mixed things up, I'd violated all the rules of taxonomy. I'd made a mess, but in the end what mattered most was Family.

I had drummers banging in my head. I had a hot oozing slash across my face. I had something that felt like a bruise on my hand, but the water was rising, so I rose, too. I made it all the way to the door that had been slammed back into its frame. I pushed with everything I had.

For a miracle of a minute, everything went still.

The door flew open, wide, and the wind slammed me in.

I dropped to my knees and my pockets spilled.

Down the hall and up the stairs, I heard that found cat crying.

24.

By the shivery light I saw it all. The Bag of Tricks beside the door beside the canes beside the shoes. The hats, the quilts, the forks, the knives, the spoons, the patchwork quilt, the *Nat Geo*s in skyscraper stacks, the early bag of candy corn that Mickey had bought the day before, stopping at the grocery store on her way home from pottery.

It's September, Jasper Lee had said.

One month from October, she'd said.

She liked a good Halloween better than anyone I know.

The flashlight lay down a line from the door to the bed, like a sidewalk through a city of hoarders. It rose like the sun toward the raftered ceiling and then dropped over curios and the couch and the adoptees from the Mini Amuse, the portrait of my aunt, the safety kit, two glass disks, which were Sterling's eyes, the stuffed walrus she'd pawed hard and chewed.

"Told you I was coming back," I shouted, so that she would hear. I thought my teeth would crack from the noise in my head. I thought the ton of storm I wore—in that coat, in my boots, in my medium hair—would drop me to the floor. I thought the split in my forehead was a bruise in my brain, and I was either raining or bleeding. I was alive, but maybe I wasn't, and I was so incredibly afraid and sad when that cat made a leaping run for me.

"Hey. Hey."

Her sandpaper tongue on my nose.

I pressed my tears into her fur. I made my confessions— I wasn't brave enough, I couldn't do enough. I needed Mickey and Jasper Lee, Deni and Eva, the entire class of the O'Sixteens, Ms. Isabel, Mr. Friedley, saying *This, too, shall pass.* Over the hurling of that storm I could hear that kitten/cat purr, I could hear her heart motoring on. I could hear her thinking: Mira Banul. Be strong.

For the both of us.

For everyone.

I lowered Sterling steady onto the bed and I fumbled until I got her a meal, and then I peeled every wet thing from my skin and wrung the deluge from my hair, pools on the floor, the storm inside, here. I crossed the room over the heads of the rescued things and dug long johns out of the top bureau drawer, my sweet pink pair, soft from a hundred years of cold Decembers. I found my best jeans and my warmest sweater and pulled on two pairs of knee-high socks. And then I found a spoon and a jar of peanut butter, and I ate it ice-cream style, chased it with candy corn, tried not to think: Mira, you're dying, or, Mira, you will be dead soon.

I remembered my phone.

Only half a bar of power left, and three missed calls, one text from Mickey:

Need to talk to you.

It was 2:18 according to the phone. I tried five times, but there was no ringing through. Power down, I thought. Save the half bar. Turning off that phone felt like another kind of losing.

25.

You'll say that what happened next could not have happened next, but it did: I slept. In the long johns, the sweater, the jeans, the socks to my knees, with my head on the walrus and my brain with the stop sign running through it, my arms full of cat, her body humming like an engine. They gave us numbers afterward—wind blow, wave rise, the deluge measured in feet and inches. My numbers were my numbers— a cat and me and the flashlight and that trench coat dripping from a hook.

I dreamed us on a cloud and in a cathedral. I dreamed us on a raft way out to sea, with humpbacks and blue whales and a manta ray flotilla and a giant, bucktoothed walrus. I dreamed the ocean full of butterflies, and the butterflies were yellow wings, and the wings were the only eyes beneath the sea. I dreamed myself a water bear, tiny monster of the sea that can survive most anything. I dreamed, and at the bottom of the ocean, there was a race down a centerline, and the eye of the tiger was winning. I dreamed, and there was a stranger with a hood in the shadow of the dark, and there was a stop sign turning over on itself, like the flicker of a horror film. I dreamed, and there were whiskers on my cheeks, there was pressure on my arm, there were two silver paws with unclipped claws kneading.

I opened my eyes.

I closed them.

I would have wished not. Not the squall, the caterwaul, the wail, the crash, not the suck-back of the waves and the starting again. Lay yourself down on a railroad track, and you'll hear a sound like those waves coming. Lay yourself down and then tell yourself this: You have no place to run.

We had no place to run.

Later, they'd give us more numbers: Forty percent of the beaches gone. Thirty percent of the houses and shops. Seven gutters dug between the ocean and the bay. Nine separate wedges of island. Eighty percent of the roads impassable.

One bridge cut down at its knees.

26.

Twenty-two thousand and two blue Slurpees.

Twenty-two thousand

and three.

27.

In the gray light of Afterward, there was crunch in my bones, the busted hinges of my knees, the bruise that had started to spill down one shin. I could also feel the leak of the volcano gurgle on my forehead. The room was spinning and it was a long time before I could sit up, inch by inch, on that bed. My eyes felt too plastic to see. I moved one hand slow across the bed. The spaces beside me were empty.

"Sterling?"

I'd puke if I moved another inch.

I didn't move another inch.

Time went in and out.

The room kept spinning.

28

Like a ship's figurehead, she sat on the heavy post of the ransacked bed.

It was the tick of her tail that I heard first—thought it was a clock, thought I was dreaming, still. Must have been infinitesimal, the sound of that tail, but that's what woke me, finally, from my own bustedness.

"Sterling?"

She heard me, leapt down, meowed. She walked a line around me, the kind they draw at murder scenes. I was the vic. She was the detective. She stopped to lick my face.

"Turned off the gas," I said, when I finally remembered some parts of some things.

Her tail went wild.

"You'll have to get yourself your own Friskies."

Her motor revved.

I pointed vaguely to the piles around us. The skyscraper stacks of my rescues. The Leaning Pisas of Banul Life as It Was. The Friskies in there somewhere, though the bag was hard to find with my plexi eyes, first day après storm.

Sterling took a long cat leap to the oak ledge of the headboard, found her footing and paced. I could hear her behind me, paw after paw, gymnast style, her toenails clacking. I closed my eyes. I heard wind in the house and gulls in the near distance. It was gray inside, but it must have been sunlight out there. Someone, I remember thinking, has to be the grown-up here.

I eased myself to the edge of the bed and uncurved my spine. I tested one foot on the spare bare clearing of the floor, then the other, and I stood. Nothing snapped. I reeled, didn't puke. There was that path between things. I walked it. Made my way to the sliding door, fit my hands around the shutter crank, fought to draw the gray light back. It took everything I had. Inch by inch, the daylight came in. It beat, like a pulse, against my eyes.

I thought I'd faint.

I steadied myself.

I looked again. The day like acid, and the world I'd known all gone.

Already the scavengers had come—the gulls greedy as pigeons, the oystercatchers with their brazen bills, an old man whose white whiskers glittered like rubble in the sun. The black rocks had been thrown like World War II tankers across the beach and tossed among them, around them, was smash: planks, tables, porch boards, rooftops, a pair of rubber tires, hangers with their dresses on, particles of window frames, a charcoal grill.

The empty shelves of a pantry.

The hats of lamps.

A chest of drawers.

A keg of beer.

My mother's apron.

My mother's apron.

The sand was a trash heap.

The sand was for pickers.

Parts of us were out there.

"Sterling?"

I opened my arms. From the headboard she flew. Her heart against my heart.

"Shhhh. Look."

Beyond the beach, bobbing in the crests and troughs of the sea, were two matching ironing boards like surfboards, and a faceup stereo, and a seagull nest, a birdbath, a teakettle, the wooden hips of a guitar, the wheel of a bike spinning like it had caught itself on a secret whirlpool. There was the swimming fin of an automobile. There was the head of the giraffe from the Mini Amuse and the feet of Wonderland's Alice, the new monsters of the sea, and now, far away, near the beach's southern end, I spied a girl throwing cartwheels where the ocean met the sand. She wore red sparkling shoes and a black leotard and a pair of ladybug wings. She cut between the surf and turned like scissors on a seam. I knew her, I thought, or I knew those wings, and then I blinked and she was gone.

Vanished.

Only Eva would be able to see.

On the deck the sand had piled like snow. The wind had torn the railings from their pins. The angle was tilt. I yanked the sliding door across its crooked tracks and the sand of the outside world fell in, across my feet, across the edge of the attic floor. Still wet. Still cool. Not warm. A gentle breeze blowing in.

"Shhhh," I told the cat. She licked my nose with her sandpaper tongue. Her whiskers like feathers against the gash on my forehead.

Through the lower half of the house I could hear the breeze blowing, and a quiet slapping like the ticking of a clock, and the sound of water falling. Sterling's ears were tall with the sound of it, too, her tail anxious. She put two paws on my shoulder. She looked past me, toward the door where I'd hooked my coat, where the pool of water wasn't as big as it had been; the water was still receding.

"Okay," I said. "All right. We'll go."

Down the narrow path. To the room's oak door.

I turned the knob.

I opened the door.

It wasn't until we reached the landing that I knew. Water to the seventh stair. The kitchen like a toilet bowl. The TV on its back. The walls between the things I could see had been erased, like chalk from a board. The curtains were down. The windows were empty. There was fish flop: flat and gray. There was the blue claw of a trapped crab, the glisten of jellyfish, like two fallen chandeliers. Every clock stopped. There was *Don Quixote* trapped in the teeth of an oven rack and a jar of mayonnaise inside a wicker basket, and I couldn't remember where things had been, how the sink had stood, where I'd left my plates, where Mickey's apron had hung, where she'd kept her calendar she'd write our histories on.

What any of it looked like, clean.

I couldn't remember, and there was a brown stain creeping up the slanted stairwell walls.

The smell was Clorox, saline, fish tail, wood rot, the fresh soil of the floating window box, chemical lemons.

The sound was the fish dying. It was the curtains drying and the ocean slinking back to the sea. It was the engine of Sterling's heart.

Go forth and conquer, Mr. Friedley would say.

Go forth.

But there was no out or through.

29.

Like being marooned in a tree house, that's how it was. The high and dry parts of the place somehow steady on their stilts, the bottom half of the house broken away. The Zone had washed out from beneath the deck, and so had everything we'd ever stuffed there, and also the dividing picket fences and the dunes and the gangplank with the rope and the footsteps from the night before, when I thought thieving was the worst thing that could happen.

There was no safe path across the crush and sludge of the first floor. There was no use in sitting on the steps watching the brown stain creep. There was no point in calling for the people I loved, because they were hours away, or blocks away, with troubles of their own, and besides, Jesus, there was no phone.

Somebody had to do something.

"Come on," I told Sterling, and she stood, her front paws on my shoulders, her bottom paws in the cup of my hand, as I climbed back up the steps and into my room and through that one thin path between everything rescued. I turned Sterling toward the bed, told her to stay, be good. I pulled my boots on, then waded out into the drifted sand, measured the distance down.

It was a freaking long way down, as if the storm had carved another full story out beneath us.

The gulls were sand gangs now—clumps of them on the driftwood chairs and in the baskets. The birdbath that had sailed out to sea had been returned to the shore, polished, its head in the sand. The old man with the whiskers was gone and if there'd been a girl wearing the ladybug wings that had once belonged to me, she'd quit her game.

There was no way down.

Even Sterling, who could fly, wouldn't dare the leap. Even Eva, hopeful as she always was, erring on the side of love, believing in the things she could not see, would have said, *The luck's not with us.*

On the prow of that deck, I knew Sterling and I had been abandoned.

The beach was like a bomb had gone off. Haven was *Lord of the Flies.* It was *Survivor.* I could see it all from where I stood.

There was no through.

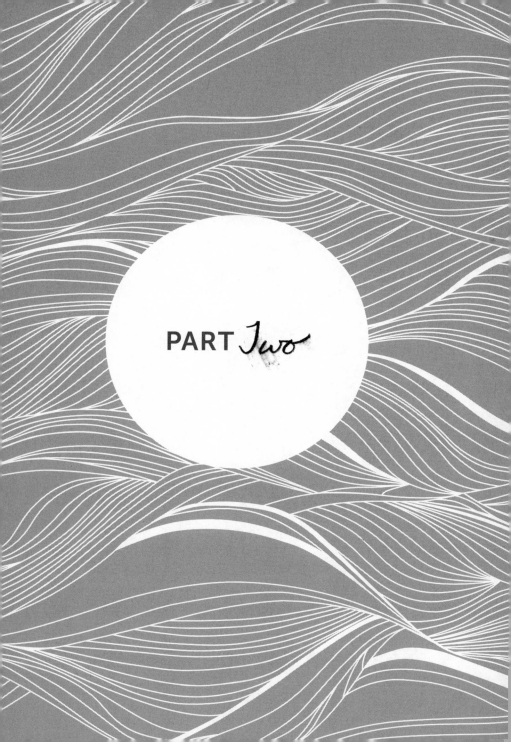

PART Two

1.

She walked heavy and slow, dragging her boots through the piles
of sand, around the banks of broken things, past the boulders.
She had a black box like a lunch pail in one hand and a
lasso of rope around one shoulder and her short hair was
as wild as hair as short as hers could be—her hair like a
Chia Pet, Kermit version. Behind her and above her, tied to
a stick, was a bright sheet flag—no hint of surrender.

Scattering the gulls, she came. Flicking her hand at
the pipers and the oystercatchers and the photographs and
diary pages and magazines that had begun to dry and lift
up, paper scatterings. The gulls were crazy as the breeze that
sometimes gusted, still, and I stood there, and she came.
That flag flapping behind her and her head down low until
she was practically under me, in the shadow of the tilted
deck, her hand like a salute over her eyes.

"Found us some rope," she said. "It should do."

Sterling leapt into my arms. Looked down. Growled
mean and threatening.

Shhhhh.

I was up on the deck, miles high, is what it seemed. She was all that distance below, the riot of the ruined beach beyond her. She made herself a seat on the pleather trunk that had drifted out and drifted back and sunk not far from home. She sat measuring rope length by the forearm and tying knots by her own degrees, her flag planted into the risen sand behind her.

I watched from up high. I watched her hands, her arms, the long length of rope turning circles at her feet. Sterling was mewing and impatient and not going any-where, because we couldn't go anywhere; we were stranded and there she was, Old Carmen, rescuing me and that cat. I couldn't understand it. I wasn't going to ask. I imagined all the others, stranded in Haven, needing in Haven, wak-ing up upside down and ruined and scared in Haven, but Old Carmen had set her compass on me. Call me selfish, maybe I was. Call me scared; I'm not pretending. Consider me banged around—body and head—and woozy with the storm. I was glad as hell to see Old Carmen. I'd have done anything she asked.

She stood now. Looked up. Said, "Now you go find yourself a decent anchor."

"Anchor?"

"You know what I mean." She threw her pointer fin-ger toward a place behind her.

I turned and looked back at the room, the insecure piles of unstable things. Only anchor in that mess was the corner post of my aunt's old bed. *No need to toss a perfectly good bed just 'cause it's ugly as sin,* Mickey had liked to say, and now, in my heart, I was thanking Mickey for looking so far ahead. I was thanking Mickey's sister for leaving me the attic room and the hurricane shutters, which were, I guess, what had saved me.

"All right," Old Carmen said. "Stand back."

"Standing."

She took her knotted rope by one end. She bundled a strong plank into it. She wound up her arm like a Yankees pitcher, and one toss was all she needed.

Old Carmen's arm was excellent.

"Anchoring it good is all on you," she said. "I'm waiting."

I retrieved the plank that had fallen at my feet. Shook off the sand, freed the end of the rope. I trudged across the deck and into that room and knotted the hell out of that bedpost. Sterling wound her silver thread between my leg as I worked. She listened to me talking, saying, "You're in on this. Be good." And then, when the knot was tight, when I had done my best, I unhooked the trench coat from the back of the attic door, slipped it on, slipped that cat into a pocket.

"You know what to do," I said.

She did. She was a real fine cat.

2.

She waited until my feet hit the ground before she asked:
"Anybody else in there?"

"No, ma'am," I said. Sterling purred.

She said, "You sure about that?"

"Yes, ma'am. Family's on the mainland."

She studied me, gauging the length of my truth. She cupped my face with the rough grip of one hand. Said, "Let's give me a look at that forehead."

I stood on that sand. I closed my eyes.

"Health," she said. "First line of our defenses."

A line from a story Deni could have penned.

She dropped my chin, reached for her black box.

3.

You want to know what she looked like. You want a closer look.

Here:

She had sea salt in her hair and a pair of tiny anchors in her ears, a Haven sweatshirt under an oiled jacket, a flannel shirt under everything. She wore a pair of jeans that ran up past her belly and tucked down straight into her camouflage waders—man-size, but they fit her. That black box of hers opened like a metal accordion, fat up to full with fishhooks and bobbins, a spare cap and bandannas, batteries, pocketknives, first aid, matches, a wind-up radio, a compass, a few paperbacks, and in one whole corner, wrapped in thick wax paper, a pile of white-bread sandwiches, smelling of salami and mustard.

She couldn't have been five foot zero.

She was almighty imposing.

Holding my chin, she swabbed my forehead wincing clean. She put a puff of gauze down where the skin had split, then a Band-Aid, tight over the seam. She asked where

I'd gotten such a nasty thing, said don't leave a wound to the elements, and then she asked me again, how, but I didn't want to remember out loud. Didn't want to remember, but the storm came back to me, its unreal power, that stop sign spinning through the howler wind.

My chin was in her hand.

Her alcohol rub was some nasty business.

"Got the gas cut off," I said.

"That right?"

"That's what they tell us in First Aid and Rescue. Get the gas turned off. I got it turned off. Then I got wind slammed."

"Bandage," Old Carmen said. "In lieu of stitches."

There were others on the beach—their long johns on, their pajama feet, their sun hats like umbrellas. They had broken things in their hands, whatever they could carry, and those gulls, they didn't like it much. Those gulls were pitching an Alfred Hitchcock fit, screaming every time somebody leaned in for the rubble, screaming like they and only they knew what to do with a broken spinning wheel or a shelf of books or the collar of a puppy but not the puppy. Knew what to do. Knew how to value.

Behind Old Carmen, the sheet-flag flew. Over her shoulder, in the direction I was facing, the Rapunzel ladder swung from the deck that was still standing, tallest thing anywhere, best that I could tell. I'd anchored the rope, and it had held. I'd left the sliding door open to the breeze.

I couldn't remember most things, or maybe I just didn't want to.

Rest of the place was a landslide smear. Roof rafters, maybe, but no roof tiles, only a handful of clapboards, and because the back door was gone you could see the splinters inside, the smashed dishes, the vertical range top, the black face of the TV laid down like a platter, and the curtains by the bay window dripping.

"You said no people inside," I heard Old Carmen saying.

"Yes, ma'am."

"No living things?"

I remembered the fish. The crab. The kelp that had hung from a lampshade, its bladders retracting like someone breathing. I remembered everything I'd tried to save, the decisions I'd made, the stash of memories, leaning.

"Not really."

"Only thing in this world isn't replaceable is people."

I nodded.

"Go on," she said. "Get what you'll need."

She folded her arms like a catcher's mitt, and that damned cat stepped right in.

She said that she would wait, and I believed her.

I fixed my hands around that rope. I clenched it with my knees. I went up again, dangled and suspended above a world of crumble.

4.

Doublewide and batteries. Peanut butter and spoon. Wallet.
Half-bar phone. Comb. Toothbrush. One canister of Viet-
namese sand and Mickey's favorite pair of earrings, color
of the sun going up. That's what she said when we gave
them to her, Jasper Lee and me. We'd walked all the way to
Main and the How to Live store, Jasper Lee leaning on both
painted canes the entire way and then also in the store:
She'd like those best. Don't cry, I told myself. Can't cry. The
candy corn, some photographs, my journal, my pen, the
cans of peaches, the cans of fish, the chips. The hairy cactus
with a Pepto bow that Eva had given me one Christmas. My
iPod shuffle with the Deni-loaded songs. The silver mug
Mickey had made for me out of a wedge of porcelain clay.
I found a duffel bag, made it fit. I tossed the tartan to the
sand below, and the walrus into the blanket, and in the
same fashion I tossed the bag of Friskies, and it went
down and down like a bomb that didn't blow, and there
Old Carmen stood waiting, my cat in her arms, like she
was a friend of mine.

Get what you'll need.

I had no one. I didn't ask questions. She had brought a flag with her and it was waving there, and it was not the color of surrender. She had patched together my head.

It was a long way to earth. The deck was dizzy. From where I stood I could see the giraffe still bobbing in the froth, the folding fingers of a music stand, the front chunk of a boat called *Mighty* something. All up and down the beach were more and more people out wearing what they'd slept in, picking their life out of the sand, out of flattened tires and laundry machines, out of the clumps of junk where the heckling gulls stood, protecting their possessions. Way out north, along the shore, I saw Chang and Mario, tall and short, walking arm over arm, slow and dazed, hardly moving forward, and I wanted to call, wanted to mold my hands into a megaphone—*Hey! Hey! Are you all right? Hey! You seen the others? You okay? Who else is there?*—but there was a mist between me and them, a mirage rising, and they didn't see me, didn't wave, like I stood on the other side of a dream. A wave rolled in carrying a machine on its back. Chang and Mario were gone, a deer standing where they'd been. A baby deer with lots of spots, dipping its hooves into the tide.

"You about ready?" I heard Old Carmen call, her flag still planted behind her and her black box at her feet, and my cat in her arms. I had no idea of next. I had no options. The deck was a prow cutting the air. The lifeline of rope was still tied at one end to the bed, still snaked across the sandy deck to the ledge, still holding.

This is what it looked like.

The shock of then.

"Cat is waiting on you," Old Carmen tilted her chin up and said.

"Sterling," I said.

She shrugged.

"Sterling. Name of my cat."

"Fair enough," she said.

I half scooted, half crab-crawled across the deck. I swept the loose sand away with one side of my hand. I got the rope up hot and alive inside my hands. Done it before, you can do it again, I said to myself. Bruised hand beneath hand, wobbly foot over foot, my head still dizzy, that bandage like a thought tourniquet, and when the breeze blew at me halfway down and I started to get vomity again, I closed my eyes and counted.

Heat of the rope in my hands, I went down to shaken sand.

"We'll have to pitch ourselves a tent," Old Carmen said.

"Tent?"

"Get ready."

Ready for what? I almost asked, and then I remembered: I wasn't asking those kinds of questions.

I threw the bag of Friskies over my shoulder. I tossed the walrus around my neck. I bundled up the blanket and tucked Sterling in a pocket, and all this time Old Carmen was plucking up her flag and folding her accordion box.

I stood with my back to her, watching the house. I stood there wondering what parts would fall next, and when, and if I'd taken the right things, and what Mickey would have done if she were here, how my little brother would have breathed.

"Moving on," Old Carmen said, and I stood there. Stuck.

"Counting on you," she said, and I had no idea why she would count on me, why she would trust me, why she would go to all that trouble with her rope.

I'm telling you.

I didn't know.

She pointed north with her chin. "Work to do," she said. "Come on."

I remember turning.

I remember fitting my boots inside her bootprints.

I remember the whisk of my trench coat across the sand.

I remember that deer, its hooves in that sea.

I remember the weight of my things.

5.

We marched until Old Carmen found a rock she liked, higher than the tide. It was up near the vanished line of the dunes, its own kind of island, with a lime green washing machine to its one side and a piano washed up by the other and a swirl of clothes still on their hangers wrapped around its base, like they were flushing down a drain. Old Carmen walked its circumference to be sure. She rubbed her fist over the rock. Then threw her black box up to the tallest part of the very tall and also quite wide rock. She stopped, before she climbed, to plant her flagpole in the sand. The flag rippled in the breeze like a kite.

No surrender.

Rock as tent.

Into one face of the rock the weather had carved four sloping steps, which is what she climbed, two at a time, her boots squeaking on the green moss, her body growing bigger the farther away she got until she towered over Sterling and me, Brothers Grimm style.

"You coming?" she asked.

I gathered the skirts of that trench coat, my bag, and climbed.

That rock was a freak-of-nature rock, big-room wide. It had its own hard shelves and troweled-out crannies and little pools where the clamshells breathed and the seaweed stoked. It was inside one of those crannies that Old Carmen would build her fire. She had climbed down the rock in search of combustibles (that was the word she used) and then returned with the dry sides of split rafters and the smashed fist of a chair and peg legs from a bed—the stuff that couldn't be salvaged, she said. The stuff the wreckers would haul off in trash trucks eventually.

I snapped the blanket out of its folds while she worked. Laid it down over the rock's black face. I arranged the spoon, the jar of peanut butter, the porcelain mug. At one end of the blanket I stuck the walrus and at the other end the cactus with the girly bow in its hair, and every time I looked up there were more people on the beach—pajama bottoms and winter coats, bunny slippers and waders, people with pictures in their hands or one of the wooden pigs from Uncle Willy's, which suddenly seemed to be everywhere—like buoys, like anchors, like what the hell?

Scenes from a zombie movie. Nobody looking like themselves. Hard to tell who was what at first, hard to put the names of the people back on the people—Mr. Xu from Liberty Bank; Jimmy D. of Paradise Custodial; Gloria Fell, who yanked your stuffed animals down from the racks at the Mini Amuse like it was the last time she'd ever be bothered; Eileen, the lady Jasper Lee and I had bought Mickey's coral earrings from and now she was traveling with a circus of curlers in her hair, mascara smudges beneath her eyes, a pair of man's chinos under a short lace dress.

I didn't want to look, felt like there was something shameful in it. Didn't want to see, wreckage like glass in my eyes, like a sailing off of hope, but I kept glancing up, my eyes blurring out with the pixilated sun, kept getting lost in my hope for them: Deni. Eva. Ms. Isabel. Mr. Friedley. Any one of the O'Sixteens—I needed proof that they were out there. Something.

Time turned on itself. Night came on. Sterling was on the rock prowl. There was a chill in the breeze, and that flag overhead. There were the flames that Old Carmen had stirred into the cranny—purple and green at first, small and nothing—until suddenly those flames sprouted and we had a fire of actual proportions. On the first night following the world's worst storm, Old Carmen and her rock were the one lighthouse. We were the rescue. We were the power.

Later, darkness fallen, somebody—too hard to know who in that dark—began to bang at the wet keys of the piano, picking a tune out of flats and sharps. Somebody tapped the orphaned keg of beer and if you didn't mind drinking lager from Dixie cups or porcelain mugs or cereal bowls, you could have yourself some. We went through

rounds of candy corn. We burnt a crust onto a dozen marsh-
mallows that somebody found in a bag; what could it hurt,
we figured, if we burnt the soggy seawater off? And then
somebody sat on top of that washing machine and started
telling stories, they were like ghost stories, and I kept looking around for my friends, kept staring into the shadows,
and my head still ached.

I was asleep with the TV on.

The voices said.

I was trying desperate to get out.

Someone.

*Goddamned forecasters. They said the goddamned thing
would pass. They said Haven was a long way from trouble.*

It was a voice I recognized, but whose? I couldn't
place it, and then it disappeared, became one note in a large
chorus:

Saved by the storm shutters.

Saved by roof rafters.

Saved by the double hill of dunes.

*Saved me? I'll tell you what saved me. The antique cra-
dle, where my grandma got rocked. Busted apart when the roof
fell in. Took me for a ride, then I rode back in. Whole house was
gone, and everything in it. But I was alive, thanks to the cradle.*

I think it's all lost. I think it is.

Some of it is somewhere.

Hell, you look around?

What are you asking for? We're all looking around.

Jesus.

Christ.

If it is somewhere, I don't know where. I sure as hell don't know what.

People who had tried to walk to Main had news: No Main. People who had gone off looking for some kind of official refuge had found: a flood in the fire station, pipes broken at the school, sand in the rescue vehicles, no higher ground. There was a tanker rammed into the face of Sea Crest Lodge, someone said, and a sail wrapped like a Christmas tree by electrical wires, and there were gulls swimming in the aisles of McCauley's grocery store, a pool in the first floor of the Maritime Museum. Somebody said that the actual lighthouse had tilted at the north end, its stripes fallen into the sea. Someone said Haven had been split into islands, thanks to the speed at which the ocean had rushed to the bay. And also, they said it over and over again: Our one bridge was gone.

Nobody knew how many had left the island ahead of the storm's worst parts. Nobody knew if there were any dead. Nobody could imagine how rescue would ever get to us, and did you see Atlantic City, somebody said, but you couldn't see Atlantic City, that was the point, because all of its lights had gone out.

Nobody said Deni's name, or Eva's. Nobody had enough of anything. Nobody could get dry, even though Old Carmen kept the fire stoked and, after a while, the only noise was the sea and the flats on the piano and the hand-cranked radio, which Old Carmen finally wrangled on— the reporters with their news, their devastating numbers, their global warnings about melting glaciers, acid skies, warming, rising, salinated, hungry seas.

By the power of the flame we listened. By the twin appearance of the moon—in the sky, low on the sea. The breeze picked up and the chill blew in and we listened, and on that Maytag people sat, and against the rock they leaned, and above their suitcases they gathered—pictures inside, valuables, a change of socks.

I looked out into the dark, past the flames on Old Carmen's rock. I told Sterling *shhhh*, I waited, anxious, for her to return when she went down into the sand, to her private business.

Old Carmen's flag rippled back and forth, in the breeze.

Her snores were like a diesel truck with a broken muffler.

I found my phone. I turned it on, its light like a fallen star in my hand. *Pleasepleaseplease*, I thought, the panic rising up again in me, the awful loud lonesomeness inside the shocked and silent crowd, but there were no bars. There was no line out to Mickey. No Jasper Lee waving back at me.

6.

Maybe you think you can't fall asleep in the bomb blast of a place that was just one e shy of Heaven. Maybe you think a rock makes for a bad bed and a stuffed walrus is a demon pillow, and maybe you've heard Old Carmen snore.

I'm telling you.

But there was a fire between her and the rest of us. The crackle of flames. I'd watched the shadows cast by the moon, and my eyes felt heavy. I'd pulled the trench coat to my chin like a blanket and Sterling had come in, soft as silk; she was not the kind of cat who would leave me cold. And after a while I wasn't shivering anymore and my teeth weren't clacking like they'd been and the bruise up my chin didn't throb as hard and I'd grown used to the butterflied wound on my head. I found some kind of music in the space between Old Carmen's snores and the sizzling of the fire and the sound of the waves carried toward shore.

I woke in the hour just before dawn. The tide had rolled in high and begun to retreat again—slide away. Through the smoke of the dying fire, I could see the giraffe way out near the horizon, empty bookshelves in the nudge of low waves, window frames, beach umbrellas, a bike built for two, its back wheels spinning. I saw the mustard-colored door of my own refrigerator, its silver handle like the fin of a marlin. I saw one half of a pair of ladybug wings.

I felt eyes on me and I turned to find Old Carmen up on one elbow, a white-bread sandwich spread on a wax-paper napkin on her chunk of the rock. She pulled her fingers through her Chia hair as a way of straightening up. Offered me half a sandwich. "No, thanks," I said, because I was busy feeding that cat with the Friskies that were left. "We're going parsimonious, Sterling," I said. "Rations from here on out."

Her whiskers, her tongue, her sandpaper nose on the palm of my hand.

"Confusion at sea," I heard Old Carmen say, and I looked out to where the sun was rising, flamingo pink, just an eyebrow of it now inside the early-morning weather. On our side of the sun six dolphins had come, slow among the floating things, testing their smells, their gravities, pushing the heavy metal around with their noses. They'd dive and then come up with a pair of argyle tights draped around their necks, a pane of curtains, a dark green Hefty bag, and then they'd shake the junk off, dive down again, scavengers hunting for a clean stretch, until the gulls were part of it, and a white crane, a stream of low-flying pipers.

I watched through the dying smoke. Old Carmen finished her sandwich. She stoked the fire. She folded the tarp she'd slept on and looked up at the flag still flying; we had survived our first night after the storm. Down below— half awake, sleep-stunned, murmuring—the survivors were wrapped up in their towels and their blankets, double hoods pulled over their heads, sand inside the tubing of their socks.

A great blue heron sauntered over the keys of the piano.

Far, far away, on the flat sand by the shore, I saw something gold, slow, sure.

I sat up. Squinted hard. I threw my trench coat on, grabbed Sterling.

"Bug in your pants?" Old Carmen asked.

"Deni," I said. "She's alive."

7.

"Tell me everything," she said. "Everything. How are you?"

She had one arm in a sling fashioned out of a towel. She had the sleeves of that army jacket cranked crooked. There was mud on both knees and a bruise on one cheek. There were tears in her eyes, and her antennae hair had been smacked down flat on her head.

She'd yanked Gem away from the tide and went full throttle when she saw me. She'd tossed one arm out of the machine and waved, frantic. "Hey! Hey! Oh my God, Mira. Hey!" She'd climbed out, then, and beelined—the stretch of sand between us like an obstacle course, both of us limping more than running; such a strange and spastic hurry.

"Jesus, Deni."

"Jesus."

"Shit."

Her voice so raspy and both of us hugging until we'd maybe break, we didn't break, we had not broken. High in my trench coat pocket, Sterling squirmed.

"That's a real fine cat," Deni said. And she burst out crying.

"Tell me everything."

This time I said it.

"Cinnamon Nose," she said. "Is missing."

She sobbed and I held her. She tried, with her story. Said her house was in one piece and one block down from its original address, a chunk of someone's kiddie pool glued to its side. Said the first floor had been soaked through but the ocean had receded, and in the dark of night, in the howling storm, they'd saved the photographs, the newspaper clippings, the hero's flag, the Reverend's favorite crosses and his best-starched collar, her brother's medal. They'd enacted the emergency plan, put it into action, shuffling and saving, step by step, and then the washing machine had torn loose from its pipes and pinned Deni to the wall, crushed her lungs, and she couldn't breathe to scream, she was dying, but her mother had saved her, dragged and kicked the machine away, tied Deni's twisted arm into a towel, kept saying, *I'm sorry*, and the water was rising and it was dark. It wasn't until Deni was on the second floor with her mom, in the three rental rooms, the saved things as tucked away as anything could be in that storm, that Deni called for Cinnamon Nose and the dog didn't come.

"I looked through all the dark and didn't see him," Deni said, describing how she'd run from window to window, opening one and calling out, "Come back here, you beautiful dog. Come back to us." But the dog was gone.

"He's nowhere, Mira. I can't find him."

Half of Deni's vowels lost to the rasp inside her throat. All of her story a heartbreak.

"Everything's chaos," Deni said.

"Complete and utter."

"World come to an end. Revelations." She sobbed. She stopped. She continued. "I kept thinking about my dad and about my brother. How neither one would stand for this. Wouldn't have let it happen. But I did."

"It was a storm, Deni."

"Shore up. Right? Shore up. I was prepared. I thought I was."

"Weather's bigger than the rest of us."

"I wanted to stop it."

"No, Deni. All of us. None of us could stop it."

She held her twisted arm with her still-good hand. She turned and looked toward the beach and all its ruin, the stumps and blasts and char. "Tell me," she said again, "everything." She touched the bandage on my head.

"Clobbered by a red octagon," I said.

"What?"

"Corner stop sign."

"For real?"

"For real."

"Jasper Lee and Mickey?"

"Still on the mainland, best as I know. Phones have all gone wonky."

I told her what I knew. I told her the size of the storm in my house, showed her the color of my bruises, which she called (of course she did) medium rare. I told her about Chang and Mario and the deer and Old Carmen, how she'd come for me with a rope over one shoulder, how she'd knotted the ladder and tossed one end to me, how she had waited, how I had climbed. Down once. Up once. Down again. I'd climbed, and Rapunzel still hung.

"Old Carmen?"

"Serious."

Deni bobbed her head as she listened. No and yes and are you shitting me, biting her bottom lip, touching the bruise on her face, coaxing her hair back up into its antennae spikes, and when she reached for Sterling, Sterling went on command—out of my pocket into Deni's hands and then up onto Deni's shoulders, where that cat sat, swiping one paw at the gulls who came too close, and now Deni was talking again, more news from her side, news on her mom, who was mostly fine, a couple of scratches from her war with the machine, a sliver of glass beneath one eye, and now back at the house that had sailed off its moorings, looking for whatever church members she could find.

"Pooling their stockpiles," Deni said. "Charcoal grills, charcoal briskets, charcoal pits, whatever there is that didn't go under." The idea of it was a community meal. The plan was to incorporate as many live human beings as anyone could find and whatever wares they could come up with— whatever was thawing in the dead freezers, whatever was floating in the pantries, whatever the gulls and the waves hadn't gotten to yet in the aisles of McCauley's.

"The plan is a meal," Deni said. "At North. The plan is to serve."

There were more people on the beach—picking and hauling, walking and dazed, zigzagging between ruptures and frames, shattered dishes, copper-bottomed pots, crab traps. The smell of things rotting.

"Total mess," Deni said.

"Total," I agreed.

"We need hope," she said. "We need—"

And I knew, and she knew, that in all our talk there was a name we hadn't said, there was news we hadn't gotten to, there was Eva, who lived in Deni's part of Haven, whom Deni would have looked for first, of whom Deni was not speaking.

"Tell me about Eva."

"I can't find her," Deni said, her voice breaking again. "I've looked," she said. "Her house is gone. It's vanished."

Nobody Deni had asked had seen Eva. Nobody had seen her parents or her two-year-old sister, Chrissy Sue, born to help save Eva's parents' marriage. Chrissy Sue was Eva's live-action doll. She had orange hair and dark brown eyes and chubby feet and fat fingers. She was the marriage solution that had not worked, Eva's parents fighting louder than before, over the baby's head, as they rocked her and fed her. And now Chrissy Sue was missing and the parents were missing and Eva was missing, but Eva missing was impossible. It couldn't be true.

The tide was swelling around our messed-up pairs of boots. My bruises were throbbing, my bandage itching. Sterling was pacing the beach by now, not going far, looking for places to do her business, because doing business, for all of us, was ranking high among the strategic nightmares. So much water on the island, but none of it useful. Haven was gooey and gross and disorganized, and it was about to get a whole lot worse, and I hope you don't mind that I will not be talking about that part of the story.

The indecency of everything.

"I have to get back," Deni said, wiping the tears from her eyes. "I promised Mom."

"Yeah."

"Meet at Old Carmen's rock later? When the sun looks like noon? A couple of hours from now?"

"Whatever hours are," I said.

"Whatever noon looks like," she said.

I needed more Friskies from the rock, more swigs of water, another meal of peanut butter. I needed the toilet that stood on the stilts of what had been my house and

I needed the supplies I'd forgotten the first time around, when my head was banged up and I was dizzy and I didn't know if I was dead and if Old Carmen was part of the dying dream I was having. I needed to climb Rapunzel and climb back down. I needed to think. I needed to figure this thing out. I needed to find Eva.

We shook on noon, Deni and I. We hugged. I kissed the bruise on her cheeks, touched her arm in the sling.

"We'll find her," I said.

We goddamned had to.

8.

It was as if time had ripped open a tomb and the dust of a million years had settled. The attic was a vague, soft thing. Sand was its only color. The stuff had blown in from the deck through the open sliding door. It had conspired and spread. It had crusted the piles I'd built and the furniture I'd inherited, coated the hook on the wall, the curl of a poster, the animals on the loveseat, the wheels of the roller skates left hanging from the lamp, the mess of clothes I'd stripped away after getting clobbered on the head. The sand had blown in, and it had won. It had claimed the things I'd saved. It was blowing, still.

Sterling leapt and slid across the slippery headboard ledge, catching herself, a startled meow. The closet door swung on its hinges, ticking like a clock. The clothes hung damp on the hangers, sand in the collars and the seams. There was the sound of the gulls in the crippled downstairs and rotting, chemical smells. I had the sense that I wasn't alone.

I wanted to run. I wanted my old cottage back, my life, my friends, my Banuls, the categories of life and living that made sense to me. Seemed like years before. Put things in their categories. Keep them known and safe.

Nothing was safe.

"Hello?"

Someone had been here. There was the trace of footsteps in the damp, crusty sand.

In the sky behind me a cloud slid over the sun. When the sun returned, I was sure: Someone had walked through the sand that had blown through the room, let their weight sink into the crystals. Footsteps—bootprints—that had walked the path I'd left between the salvage I'd collected. There were footsteps, and there was proof, too, of a person having lain down on my bed—something about the way the sand was scattered from the pillow, something of a trace of long legs and strewn arms in the horizontal sheets of sand. The doors to the curio cabinet had been left open, but not by me. That swinging closet door wasn't right, I'd heard the latch latch before I'd rappelled to the beach that first time, Sterling in my pocket. The drawers to my bureau had their tongues hanging out, and I had not left those tongues hanging out. And now, I realized, some of the piles I'd built had been rearranged—divided and restacked, cut through and repositioned. Breezes stirred in the crusty pots and pans. Air rustled inside the old news of magazines, and when the next breeze blew the wings snapped. There was a rise of crisp, white birds.

"Hello?" I said.

The boots had walked the skinny path in the hoarder's city and returned. They had stepped back over the threshold of the sliding door and trailed away through the ever-shifting sands on the tilted deck. Hello to no one. Whoever it had been was gone. He'd cut across the deck and slid the rope Old Carmen had thrown and I'd secured. He'd slipped away, onto the beach, where everything was chaos and the rules had been tossed and nothing was like it had been before, and there was something in his pockets. Or might have been.

He'd taken, or he hadn't.

He'd be back, or he was satisfied.

He'd been looking for something.

Or he'd found it.

Someone had come. Someone had gone. Whatever had been taken was infinitesimal when stacked up against all that had been stolen by the storm. The breeze would blow the stranger's bootprints from the sand. The tide would convert the evidence. There was no one but me who could ever be sure that he'd climbed up, walked through, lain down on my bed, but I knew, and Sterling's whiskers were on alert, and I remembered, as if it had happened in another world, the thief who had crept in and out of the Zone.

Now with the next breeze another flight of crisp, white birds flew—lifted up from the split stack of *Nat Geo*s

I'd saved. They were paper birds, pages sailing out of my brother's magazines. I reached for one. I turned it over. I read my brother's words.

This is the story of you:

Stuff: Forams
      Chabazite
      Olivine
Source: Kapalua, Maui
Ordered: May 8, 2011
Received: July 2, 2011
Fact: Smitherings are lovely.

Smitherings are lovely.

"Jasper Lee?"
I reached out into the breeze. I snatched the next white bird. I read.

This is the story of you:

Stuff: Sea urchin spine (red)
      Sea urchin spine (green)
      Coral dust
Source: Galápagos Islands
Ordered: March 3, 2013

Received: April 16, 2013
Fact: What you are is still alive.

I sat on the bed, on the shivering sand, where the stranger had lain down before me. I heard Sterling mew and leap. I felt her find my lap. I felt her paws insist, ask questions. There was another crisp, white paper bird now, close enough to snatch. I read:

This is the story of you:

Stuff: Pink garnet
  Green epidote
  Red agate
  Black magnetite
  Hematite
Source: Lake Winnibigoshish, Minnesota
Ordered: November 2, 2012
Received: January 4, 2013
Fact: You will always be your own true colors.

One by one the pages that used to be stuffed inside the stack of Nat Geos peeled away, and one by one, I reached for them and read them. The story of sand scooped out of a war. The story of sand from a blackened beach. The story of diatoms and shark-tooth shatters. The story of something wanted, asked for, mailed—mollusks, coral, barnacles, basalt, foraminifera. The stories were of crush and time. They were of broken beauties, missing pieces, legends. They were the stories of sand and the story of my brother. They were somebody crying. They were secrets. They were chasing each other with every breeze that blew in, and Sterling was quiet now, touching her paw to each page, tracing the clumsy letters that my brother had written in the blackest charcoal.

All glory to the survivor.
Live eternal.
Invisible is not the fault of the thing,
but the fault of the person who's looking.

"Jesus," I said.
"Jasper Lee," I said.
And I don't know if I've ever missed a human being as much as I missed him.

9.

The nicking of the sand blowing in.

The cat on my lap.

The cries of gulls in the empty space beneath me.

I closed my eyes.

The sand sifted, stayed.

I remembered.

Something.

10.

An adventure we'd had. It was a December Sunday, Mickey sleeping in. It was the voice on Old Carmen's radio reporting snow coming in from the north. Old Carmen out on the rocks, wrapped in her blankets, her radio blaring, her flag at her back.

"I would prefer," Jasper Lee had said.

"Prefer what?" I'd asked.

We'd been lying feet to feet on his double bed, watching the planes fly nowhere above our heads. I had my hands beneath my head. He was propped up on three pillows. Around his mouth were the triangle lines from the BiPAP machine he had slept with—the face mask leading to the tubes leading to the machine on wheels, the machine's green face glowing. He'd needed the BiPAP air the night before—more oxygen into his stunted lungs, into his blood—but now he was breathing on his own. He had his glasses on, the ones with the lavender frames. His eyes were open. And then they closed.

"I would prefer to be the first Year-Rounder to see the year's first snow." He said it all at once, with a single breath, then took a noisy swallow of air.

"That's what you want?" I said.

"That's what I want," he said.

It was quiet in the house, with Mickey still sleeping.

He cranked his one foot around its anklebone. I heard the bones in his body pop. He sighed and his lungs gurgled and I pretended I didn't hear—studied the ceiling, thought about the things my brother preferred. To find the stars on a clean-sky night. To have a second scoop of ice cream, just before bed, teeth already brushed. To have somebody read him his favorite books, over and again. To be photographed sitting so no one could see the curve of him standing, or not to be photographed at all.

I was lying there imagining that I could see us both from up above, that I was flying one of his planes, looking down. My head at his footboard, my knees like a tent, the shine on my painted toenails, the flop of Jasper Lee's tube socks, the crank of his foot, his flannel pajama bottoms with their rolled-up hems, the Yankees sweatshirt that Mickey had hemmed quick with a pair of scissors and some yellow thread. I imagined Jasper Lee's hands, like animal hands, he used to say, like claws. I imagined his head propped high on three foam pillows. I imagined his nose, his lips, his tongue as what they were, and after that, his ears, which were perfect pale, exotic shells.

The enzymes had not touched them.

Through the windows behind him, I could see the nighttime dialing its darkness back. To the one side was the BiPAP. To the other his nightstand with the home-schooling pile—the workbooks and secondhand Scholastic readers and science that Ms. Isabel sent home once each week in a green-folder pack, Ms. Isabel staying sometimes, sitting on the edge of Jasper Lee's bed explaining, or asking Mickey for baking soda and setting off a volcano, or listening to Jasper Lee talk about his sand, because already he had questions about its infinitesimalness, about how there was so vastly much, how the world never ran out of sand. Ms. Isabel listened. She helped him look things up. She brought him books, she brought him vials, she drew out worksheets just for him.

Everything was frozen beside Jasper Lee's bed.

Everything was still.

Jasper Lee wanted to see the snow.

It was like a dream he'd had.

"All right," I said, after a long time. "All right. Get up."

He struggled up onto his elbows, didn't understand.

"Be ready," I said, "for when I come back." I rolled off the bed and left him where he was. I ran the stairs to my room, but very quiet. I turned on no lights. I hurried into my jeans. I pulled one of my aunt's old hats and scarves from the closet we shared and pulled my skates from beneath the skirt of the bed.

He was ready by the time I got back downstairs. He was standing by the door with his four-pocket khaki pants on, the hems cuffed high. He had his navy parka on and

Mom's tulip-patterned scarf around his neck and his straw hat pressed to his head, his lavender glasses on the bridge of his stunted nose.

"Game on," I said, opening the door, letting it close soft behind us.

He waited. I got ready. Fit the skates onto my Skechers. Took the key from around my neck. "Wheels up," I said at last, crouching so that he could climb onto my back—tie his arms around my neck, knot his legs around my waist. Our house was four miles from Haven's northern tip. Jasper Lee was seven years old and small and weighed what I could carry. I was his sister, and together we were strong. I felt his heart beating into my left shoulder blade.

I walked over the pebbles.

I stepped onto the walk.

I climbed over the curve.

We were off.

All the pebbled lawns of Haven were sleeping, and Mickey, too, was sleeping, and the darkness was giving way to gray, and we disturbed no one. We reached the north end of the island just as the snow began to fall.

"What you prefer," I said, catching my breath. "At your service."

He hugged me hard from behind, and then he climbed down. I skated, he slowly walked to a weathered bench where the fishermen sat on summer days, throwing their lines into the sea. But that day it was just Jasper Lee and me keeping company with the striped lighthouse and the lapping edge of the water and the soft snow that fell. We let it fall on us, gently blanket us, color of perfectly white and simply perfect.

"You're the luck part of my life," he said. "You and Mickey and Haven."

11.

The luck part of his life, I thought. The luck part of something. I'd been sitting on the bed where the stranger had been. The sand had been breezing against me, a stiff crust. Sterling had settled in for a nap and so had the crisp, white birds of Jasper Lee's stories. I didn't know the time, but the sun was higher. Deni would be coming for me soon, standing by Old Carmen's rock, anxious with news—her news to tell and to take.

I used the toilet down the hall that didn't flush. I dug out my map of Haven as it once had been, before all its parts had perished, the thermos that had rolled beneath my bed the night of the storm, still some water in it, and these I tucked into my trench coat pockets, alongside Jasper Lee's stories. I did all this, but first I found the pen and journal I'd salvaged the day after the storm, still right there in my trench coat pocket. I wrote:

Tell me who you are, and what you're taking.

"Game on," I told Sterling, nudging her out of her sleep and tucking her down into the pocket. I found a snow globe in the curio cabinet. I left the note on the bed. I anchored it down with the snow globe.

That was it. All my preparations.

"Let's blow this popsicle joint," I told that cat, and we staggered out, across the tilted deck. We gave our lives over to Rapunzel.

12.

The tide was drawing back. The sand was wet cement oozed over gutters, swished across ironing boards, flat on the flat-screen TVs, swirled in the swirls of chandeliers and candle-sticks. The beachcombers were scavenger birds, their heads bent, their hands hooked over cranky parts and pieces. Nothing had changed except the smell was worse and the beach seemed more crowded and there were bootprints, somewhere, left behind by the stranger who'd come, kicked up into the chaos.

The sun was noon-high in the sky. I picked my way toward Old Carmen's rock—the red flag flapping and the fire sending up a thin SOS. The hem of my trench coat skittered over the dry upper sand. It dragged where the sand was damp and my waders sank. Sterling had two paws on my shoulder and her tail in a pocket. She had assigned herself a detail that I called the reverse lookout.

"You are," I told her twice, "an excellently fine cat." She was especially talented in reverse.

Now, lifting one hand to block the sun, I searched for Deni. I saw everything but her and nothing but ruin. I kept walking, watching where my waders went, cutting the distance between me and the rock, until finally I saw Deni still way out there, hugging the shoreline in her brother's army boots. Her hair had spiked back up to antennae heights. Her aviators were pooling the sun. She'd changed into her brother's ARMY sweatshirt, its round neck cut in a fraying V—I would have known that anywhere, picked it out from any mile—and she was traveling Gem-free. Her hurt arm high in its sling, she was half-walking, half-running; she hadn't seen me.

"Hey!" I waved.

Too much between us.

Matching Deni's pace now, ignoring the throb in my knee, threading as quickly as I could across the stalagmite landscape. I was doing a dangerous weave between sofas and butcher blocks, pillows and lampshades, the people I knew, the split side of a deck, the triple shelves of a library shelf, Elly P. in loafers and an anchor miniskirt, Rahna D. with a bandanna holding back the lovely masses of her hair, Dr. Hagy, who had never gone far without her tennis racquet and who was carrying it now, like a miniature webbed table, its strings holding the silverware she had dug out from the sand. We all were going in between and out. We were stopping to hug each other, to console each other, to say what we'd heard, what we knew, what we suspected, but not for long. We had to carry on. We were scratched, dirty, standing, sorry, and there was nothing we could do, and Deni was coming, she was so much closer, and when people wanted to talk I did, and when people couldn't look up I understood.

Tragedy is a public thing.

It is also a private condition.

"Hey, Deni!" I called, and she heard me this time. Stopped to make sure. Started cutting faster in my direction. She was past Old Carmen's rock, her boots splashing the edge of the sea. She was past where the deer had been and where Chang and Mario had disappeared into the mirage or into the weird place of my imagination. Weather vanes and a parking meter and a Christmas wreath lay tossed between us. A chili bowl, a clothesline pole, a telephone, a mattress. The mattress had its quilt intact and a wet dog curled at its end and I thought it was dead except for how it barked when we passed, and now Sterling was making a show of discontent—little desertion moves, all four of her feet crouched on my shoulder.

"Don't you dare leave your post," I said. "We're almost there." Lifting her from my shoulder to give her a good, stern glare and still walking forward because Deni had news, I could tell she did, and I had news for her.

That's when the thud of my boot struck the bell of some metal.

That's when I tripped and shivered forward, then fell flat.

I remember Sterling flying, better than some circus act.

13.

She was helping me up to my elbows. She was yanking the trap off my foot. She was pulling off my wader, measuring my ankle with one hand.

"What the hell?" I said.

"Not swollen," she said. "At least not yet."

The sky a little too blue. The clouds were fuzzy.

"Ms. Isabel," Deni explained. "Her roller cart."

I sat up a little higher, let the next wave of dizzys pass, let my eyes focus, and Deni was right: It was Ms. Isabel's cart—mangled and empty. Ms. Isabel's cart that I'd stepped inside and that had snapped its jaws like a land mine.

"Look," Deni said now. She stood and came back with a busted cassette player in one hand, its lid cracked to ninety degrees. She stood again and scooped a tangle of coppery magnetic tape from not so far away. It looked like tumbleweed, or a strand of yarn. It looked like play to Sterling.

Deni waited for my queasiness to fade. She watched Sterling bat the magnetic tape, all those vanished birdsongs. She looked at me and brushed her fingers across my forehead. "Looks like you fell asleep facedown in a pile of sand," she said. "You should be careful. That thing on your face could get infected."

I would have told her right then about the stranger. I would have asked for her advice, but right then I didn't know how to. She'd done her evaluation on me, and I was dirty but I'd be fine. "Give me your hand," she said, pulling me up with her one good one.

We stood side by side, surveying the world at our feet.

"Pompeii has nothing on this," she said.

And then: "I still can't find Eva."

14.

The news from North wasn't good. Deni told me as we walked. Five dead of drowning. Seven dead of crush, shock, or heart attack, bad luck, worst choices. Several dozen unaccounted for and six whole blocks of North gone, no proof that anyone had ever lived there to begin with. Without the bridge and with so many slips and ships sunk off the mainland itself, it would be days before the National Guard could come, the police and medics, the unlocal firemen.

"I can't find Eva, Mira." Deni said it again.

We'd been back to the rock. Filled two pockets with Friskies, nodded at Old Carmen, who had nodded at us, who had moved the cactus with the pink bow from one end of the rock to the rock's very middle, near the shine of her toolbox. *Deni Norfleet,* Deni had said, putting her hand out like she'd been trained to do, cause and effect of her status as a minister's daughter. Old Carmen shook Deni's hand back, like they were making a pact: two survivors who thought things through better than the rest of us.

"Broken or sprained?" Old Carmen asked, about Deni's slinged-up arm.

"Sprained, ma'am."

"You keep it protected. No messing around."

"No, ma'am."

"You tell this one"—Old Carmen pointed at me—"to keep that bandage clean on her head. Cut like that, it takes some healing time."

Deni looked at me and nodded. Told Old Carmen she was heading out for some reconnaissance. Nobody but a girl in her brother's shipped-home uniform could have used that word straight, but it fit Deni fine.

Old Carmen nodded. Deni did a salute. No questions needed between two people who took defense as their first duty.

We left the rock and headed west toward what used to be the town, Sterling trotting behind us. The asphalt, the sidewalks, the former yards of former houses were somewhere and somehow beneath us, but really: Haven was sand. Haven was an unending stretch of Jasper Lee's obsession, far and wide as our eyes could see. I needed quiet to take the strangeness in and some privacy to look away. I needed a different kind of map.

"Used to be—" I said.

"No looking back," Deni said. She shook her head.

The sure corners and right angles of the town equaled gone. The telephone poles stood at slugger angles, the wires strung between them loose and low as black *U*s. Street signs and shop signs were tossed notes; I thought of the flying octagon, the crack in my head. It was as if asteroids had fallen from the skies and this time it wasn't H_2O but glass and timber, Plexiglas and metal, cash registers, frying griddles, the ice cream cases from McCauley's, brass doorknobs and plates.

"This way," Deni said.

I thought again of the useless map. Sterling lagged behind, trotted ahead, let her tongue hang loose and her tail wag and her triangle ears poke high anytime we stopped, anyone we saw, anybody Deni asked: *How bad are you hurt? What do you need? Heard about the brigade at North? Seen our other best friend, Eva?*

"Eva Hartwell," she'd say. "Platinum blond? About so tall?"

She'd wave the photo that she'd tucked inside her pocket: *Show me where.* Hunch her shoulder on account of that sling, on account of needing to know.

Anybody Deni asked knew Eva—*The pretty girl, the delicate one, the one whose mom would sing at Buckeye's on Fridays, that one? Yes. Eva Hartwell. Haven't seen her since the storm. A brigade at North? What kind of brigade? Who else have you found? Who has a radio?*

Minister's daughter, hero's sister—that was Deni. Polite. Determined. *Please.* But we couldn't find Eva in the gutters of Main, in the broken crosswalks, in the humps of sand, in the cars with their windshields torn off, on the buried steps of Alabaster, in the Slurpee freezers that had been tossed to the street, in the questions Deni asked. *Eva?* We walked until our feet felt like a color—blue. We walked and we would not stop because we had to find Eva, because she was waiting on us, because no more losses were acceptable; the storm had stolen enough. Because Deni said, *How about the sanctuary?*, which was a crooked block that way, and because we went.

We were searching for Eva.

We walked side by side plus cat between houses that had tossed their coats to the ground, their underthings. Houses standing around in their bones with their roofs peeled off, torn curtains like petticoats in the windows, broken glass in the yards, which were heaped sand. Nobody out. Nobody home. Keep walking. Until we reached the crushed shells of the sanctuary lot, which we could not hear or feel, because they were buried beneath sand.

Deni kept going. Sterling climbed up into my hands. No boardwalk, no rope rails, no dragonflies up ahead. No Respect. No Preserve. Just ruin. "Eva!" Deni called. "Eva!" The unearthed roots of the sanctuary bushes squirming like worms. The trees split or in a crouch, the paths plugged or destroyed, and I stood there trying to remember before, the O'Sixteens, the darted wings of birds, Eva and Shift in the easy shade, the pop quiz Ms. Isabel wouldn't have had the heart to give us.

"She wouldn't have come here," I told Deni. "Why would she come here?"

"Because she's Eva," Deni said, and I knew what she meant: heart for a head. Alabaster romantic. *I can see Alexandria from here. I can see Last Island. I can see vanishing, and maybe I can stop it.* She'd been last seen with Shift, that was all we knew, and who was he, and where had she gone?, and where were the birds?; the trees had lost their heads. It was silent, too silent. Nothing stirred except for the twigs Deni snapped, the nests we walked on, the whisks of ourselves through the claustrophobic leaves.

"Eva!" Deni called, as we made our way through the jungle of the place, but it was useless. The broken stumps and fallen limbs kept taking us back to where we started until Deni would begin again and I would follow and I began losing sight of that short hair, that fraying sling. With every whip-back of the branches I was confused. With every turnstile churn of the splintered trees. With every step through the scuttling green, the thorns.

Deni went deeper and I followed and Sterling kept her head tucked low and sometimes, through a break in the trees, the sun would shoot through and I would go blind or dizzy or more confused. "Deni?" I called, because I couldn't see her anymore, and I stopped, and there, in the wishbone split of a broken tree was a kite, but it wasn't a kite, it was half of a bird. The single wing of a swan.

"Deni?" I called.

"Eva!"

I heard her.

The branches. The brambles. The shadows. The buzz, low to the ground and suddenly, up ahead, it went perfectly still. No more boots crunching fallen things. No more *Eva* echoing back. I heard something in my own heart snap. I heard Sterling *grrrrrrrr*.

"No, no no no." I heard Deni's voice at last. "No!"

I battled the limbs. I ran.

I saw the long coat first. The lavender. The buttons. I saw the tossed book with its green spine cracked, its bird wings fading. I saw the everlasting dreads and the oak where Shift had been sitting a few days before, Shift and Eva, together and strange, but now the oak was sawed in half and its top branch had crashed, and beneath it—her eyes wide and her body still—lay Ms. Isabel.

"Help her," Deni was saying. "Help me." Taking Ms. Isabel's pale hand in hers, scrunching down to turn her head, find her mouth, blow air into the empty lungs. It sounded like drowning—Deni sobbing into Ms. Isabel's lungs. I yanked at the fallen limb, scratched at the bark, desperate to relieve the killing weight of things. I couldn't. Nothing moved. Not the limb, not our teacher's lungs.

The branches and the brambles like a roof against our heads.

The terrible misting of bugs.

Sterling on the ground, mewling.

"Ms. Isabel," Deni was crying, rocking back, rocking forward. "We're here, Ms. Isabel. We're right here."

There were rivers running down Deni's cheeks. There was desperation in the way she moved, until suddenly she stopped and threw herself against the stump of the murderous tree, and I was thrown back with her. I tried to imagine Ms. Isabel in the dark of the storm, in the terrible winds, the deafening howl. I tried to imagine, but I couldn't stop the sky from falling. I couldn't fix anything. It was Ms. Isabel who had come, not Eva. Ms. Isabel who had died for the birds.

What are our responsibilities? A Ms. Isabel question.

To pay attention.

To love the world.

To live beyond ourselves.

How much time went by? I don't know. How could we stand it? We couldn't. How are we alive, still? Parts of us aren't. I couldn't see, for all those tears. I couldn't breathe, for all that sadness. I couldn't. When I looked up again I saw the break of sun between two dented limbs, I saw a slow heartbeat in the trees. I heard a deep *whoosh* and I saw a dagger and a beard of feathers.

A deep *whoosh whoosh*, and then it flew.

"The great blue heron," I said, and Deni looked, too.

The Bird will make sure that all things are put in their proper places on earth.

"Proper places," I said.

And there was no counting all those tears.

15.

I talked to Mickey and Jasper Lee. I talked to Mr. Friedley and the O'Sixteens. I talked out loud, I talked inside, I said, *I am sorry but maybe I'm not big enough for this, not brave enough, not strong enough.*

Deni talked to her dad. Deni prayed. She promised another perfect person on her way to heaven. "Make room for more wings." Her tears like two rivers and mine like the seas and we closed Ms. Isabel's eyes. We buttoned her coat. We made a bouquet of white swan feathers. We slipped them into her dreads.

"We need to tell someone," Deni finally said. A choke of words. A respectful decision.

She stood tall as she could beneath the ruined trees.

"I'll go, you'll stay? You'll keep her company?"

"Of course."

"I'll—"

She tried to speak but couldn't.

"You won't be long," I said.

"Coming back," she said. "Soon. For Ms. Isabel."

16.

Once, a very long time ago, I was drowning. I'd gone out for a
swim. I was nine years old. It was dark, and I should have
been sleeping, and Jasper Lee was just a toddler then who
cried at night; there was no name for his disease. Mickey
was four part-time jobs and exhausted and she had sung
him to sleep, like she always sang him to sleep, and on this
night, I remember, she fell asleep beside him, on his bed.

The ocean was right there. Down the stairs, through
the Zone, over the lump of the dune. The tide was high. I'd
been sitting on my deck chair listening to the lather foam,
my skin sticky with sea-salty sweat. I only wanted a swim. It
didn't seem so wrong. My bathing suit was dry on the deck
rail, and the sea was right there, and I pulled my T-shirt
and my underpants off, put my tank suit on. Mickey didn't
hear me on the stairs going down, didn't hear my feet out
in the Zone, over the Dune, on the night sand. I felt the first
foam on my toes and waded deeper in.

A cool splash.

A knee dip.

Ocean to my thighs.

The moon was a few days after full. The stars were bright as planets. I lifted my chin to see the million pinpricks, and then I lay on my back to count them. It was so easy, lying there on the pulsing waves, easy as sleep in a cradle. My medium hair swimming from my medium face. My arms and legs wide, like a starfish.

I was too young to know the power of the tide. I was too in love with the magic of the stars to think about the shore, to gauge my place in the sea. I was too slow to realize that the depth beneath me had changed and the waves were riding higher and now there was something up against the flesh of my neck, something nipping at my hair, a tug. I stood to shake myself clean, but there was no sand beneath me. I was out too far, suspended like a puppet from its strings in the bob of the sea, and the waves were drawing me out, farther.

Farther.

Farther.

There was no one near to save me.

I flung myself toward the shore, but my body tugged under. I dove, I rose, I drifted. The more I tried, the worse it was—the water pulling me down, the lights along the beach growing tiny as the stars, the picket fence, the dune fading from view. I screamed, and I was sinking. I called out and my words were bubbles. I batted my arms and kicked my legs and my body pulled me down.

Waves breaking.

Waves over my head.

We die backward. That's what I learned that night. We die looking over the length of our own lives, floating through time. I saw Mickey singing to my brother in his bed. I saw Mickey stacking the plates in the sink. I saw Jasper Lee with his blue bucket on, king of the tidal parade. I saw the day I'd moved into the attic room—*It's yours now, sweetie, all this and the view, too*—and the birthday party with the sequined wings. I saw me at three and Deni at three, Deni with long, glossy hair, no aviators; I saw Eva blowing out candles. I heard Mickey saying, *You're a big girl now,* and I heard her crying, and the last thing I remember is feeling very sad, feeling sinking, feeling sad, and everything bobbing up and down and the stars losing their light and I wasn't afraid after that.

All gone.

All done.

Good night.

And then it was all dark and all right until my back was thrown hard against the sand, until my lungs exploded with salty air, until water poured like fire through my nose until I thought I heard, somewhere far off, a song. Time changed direction. Mickey's fists were pounding my lungs, her mouth was feeding mine air, I was sicker than I'd ever been.

"Don't you ever do that again," she sobbed. "Never. Ever. Ever."

I looked up, and Mickey's hair was like yarn. Her tears were like dewdrops. Far away I thought I heard the sound of someone leaving.

"Don't ever," she repeated. "Again."

I looked down the beach, in the direction of the footsteps and thought I saw, never knew if I saw, a shadow trailing off.

Mickey would speak of it no more. She blamed herself.

"Come back," I whispered to Ms. Isabel. "Please."

But there on the pine-needle ground our teacher did not move. There with the feathers woven into her hair and her coat buttoned so that she wouldn't grow cold and Sterling watching over her, batting the insects away, and a single dragonfly had come, and from somewhere I couldn't see, a bird had started to sing, and beside that song was the *whoosh whoosh* of the heron. The survivors of the sanctuary. Us.

Home of the brave, I thought. Home of the brave. I wrote Ms. Isabel like my brother would. I wrote her down, for Eva's eternal ever.

Stuff: The black bird with the red wings.

The blue heron in the green shade.
The swan that wanted to save you.
We wanted to save you,
Too.
Bird chirp, wing beats, owl lullabies,
Kites and nightjars, hummingbirds,
Also dragonflies.
Source: Every song that played the skies was
Something
You knew.
We knew,
Too.
We'll know
Always.
Lost: September 20, 2015
Fact: This is the story of you.

"The story of you," I whispered.
I kissed her cheek.
I watched her sleep.
"Don't be afraid," I said.
"We won't forget you," I promised.

17.

That night, on Old Carmen's rock, I could not sleep. I closed my
eyes and it was all right there. The lavender coat. The shattered limb. The broken shade. The dragonfly. The heron.
Ms. Isabel, the story of her. Deni returned, but I don't know
when. She returned with the people she had gathered—
Miss SaraBeth, Mr. Samuel Brown, Darlene Daniels, Jeffrey
Bean, one of them a lawyer and one of them a friend and
one of them, Darlene, in a big straw hat and a quilt in her
hands. It took all of us to shove the fallen limb away. All
of us to lift Ms. Isabel's body into the sling of the quilt, and
to carry her one final time through the hovering trees.

Respect. Preserve.

Like a dream.

Like a death.

I couldn't sleep.

The fire on the rock pressed its heat against my back.
My clothes stunk of tears. Sterling's fur was in my pockets.
The trench coat was tucked to my chin. I nested my head

on the walrus pillow. I told Sterling to come, and she did. Put the motor of her heart alongside mine. Raised her tail.

"Come with me," Deni had said, before she'd turned north for her house, for the brigade. "Come with me. There's room."

I shook my head.

"Brigade up there," she'd said, all those tears still in her eyes, her skin pale, her bones shaky, her arm and her heart in a sling. "My mom. There's room."

"Eva needs you at North," I'd said. "She needs me at Mid. We still have to find her."

Because we hadn't, not yet. We'd found the story of Ms. Isabel, the story of Haven in the smashed-in pools and the twisted teeth of silverware and fishhooks. We'd found new beards on old men, and women whose hair frizzed like bad wigs, and people we knew wearing other people's coats, and Steffy Gomez with a sled behind her, pulling her perfect microwave like it was her one and only possession. We could not lose Ms. Isabel and we had. We could not be apart from the people we loved, but some of them were distant, some of them were far away in a hospital, where everything depended on the generators working, the water being clean, the doctors staying on call, the mother and the brother willing. Where everything had to be all right—it had to be. I couldn't go on if it was not, so I assumed what had to be.

We needed Deni at North and me where I was—both of us scanning the huddles, watching the tide, looking for a sign of our best friend, her big, good heart, her capacity for seeing. Tomorrow I'd get up and step down and walk into the sea and wash off everything that hurt me. I'd walk south toward the ruin of the cottage and climb the rope. I'd fortify, keep hunting.

Nobody else was allowed to die.

No more losses.

Period.

I'd be the hope. I'd be the heron. I'd do a goddamned something.

We had to find Eva.

The lights of Atlantic City were still dark. The stars were bright as planets. The moon was a little smaller than it had been. On Old Carmen's radio they were telling the news like they had it—calls coming in from battery radios, helicopters flying overhead, White House sorrows. There were numbers and percentages. There was desperation along the coast. The power was down, the water was mucked, fires were burning, buildings had fallen, people were trapped, and the governor would be a long time coming. The barges, medics, firemen, the National Guard, the bulldozers that could dig us out, the armada we needed—it was all far away, still. It was en route. *Patience,* the voice on the radio said, and someone just beyond the big rock groaned, and nobody—no reporter, no eyewitness, no passing bird or cloud—had a word to say about Memorial.

Old Carmen turned the dial.

The voice went dead.

I fed Sterling. I ate some peanut butter. I heard that strange song on sticky keys. I lifted my head and squinted into the flickery dark. I could see the armchair that had been dragged across the sand and left by the piano. I could see the outline of a person sitting there, hands like light rags at the end of dark sleeves. The song sounded like boots walking through rain, like no song I'd ever heard. I stared at it hard, listened. I heard the heartbeat of a heron flapping in.

"Best thing for you would be some sleep," I heard Old Carmen say.

I turned toward her, the fire between us, the pink bow on Eva's cactus getting singed. Old Carmen's knees were up, her fingers laced beneath her head. I could see the crab traps on the rock behind her, the metal cubes she'd tossed into the sea all afternoon, standing there with the tide up to her knees. She'd put the crabs into a cast-off iron pot and carry the pot up the rock steps to her fire. She'd boil the crabs in seawater, snap off one leg, test the taste, agree with it, until soon there were others working the crabs with her—finding pots and pot lids, dishes and forks, ways to feed whoever had come to live and sleep near the rock. She had listened to the news about our teacher. She had put her powerful arm around me. She had shaken her head and a tear had fallen down and she had said, "Take this rock. Do your grieving."

Then she had climbed down the four stone stairs and called out to the others, as if Ms. Isabel's death had left her even more resolute to do more to save Haven at Mid.

You all have something, Old Carmen had said, *that you can contribute.*

We can't do this, she'd said, *alone.*

She talked until the people stopped what they were doing. Until they looked up and listened. Until they were persuaded. Until they stood. Boxes of Pop-Tarts. Jars of jam. Granola bars. Containers of raisins. Planks of wood found steaming in the sun. Washed-up tablecloths that had caught the breeze and dried. It was as if Old Carmen were the mayor, the superintendent, the chef. It was as if her rules were the only rules—her instructions on crab, her arrangements of things, her ideas on barter and trade—a crab for a box of salt, a crab for a bunch of bananas that had washed up, ripe, a crab for something somebody needed more than the person who had found it—except that Old Carmen was keeping nothing for herself. *Community pantry.* Woolgathering for the days we'd have ahead, and she had the fire, she had the radio, she had the ideas, and they said yes.

She'd left me on that rock. She'd left me, let me be, watched, I think, I know for sure now, as I curled into a fist and sobbed. We had to survive because others hadn't. We had to grieve the countless losses. She'd form the brigade at Mid, she'd do what she could, more than she was already doing. I heard her up on the rock, felt the stoking of her fire, heard her No Surrender flag rippling the breeze. I felt her touch my shoulder. I turned.

Best thing for you would be some sleep. I almost asked her then why she had come for me, why she had shared her rock with me, why I was the one out of everyone who had a fire to sleep with, her rope to climb down, her ration of bottled water to share. We had ignored her for all those years. She'd been as invisible as a larval blenny fish. We had left her to the weather and to the sea and she hadn't been a Vacationer and she hadn't seemed a regular Year-Rounder and some had said that maybe she was crazy and all of us had called her old, but she had to have been young once, she could not have been, forever, Old Carmen. She had come to me, she had waited for me, she had saved me, and I could not save Ms. Isabel. And I might have asked her right then:

Why me, Old Carmen? Why?

What is the logic of rescue?

But I had Ms. Isabel's dying on my mind. I had Eva missing and Mickey and Jasper Lee gone and somebody stealing from the cottage that had broken apart, and if I'd asked her, she might have told me, and I might not have been strong enough for the answers she had.

Sleep. That's what she said. There was the song like the boots-inside-the-rain and the tapping of fingers on the Maytag. There was the sound of the fire on the rock. There was the crash of the waves against the sea of broken wings and the heartbeat of a heron.

If I slept, I dreamed. If I dreamed, my dream was Ms. Isabel, high up now, and flying, the bright beam of my doublewide pointed toward the sky, connecting dots from earth to star—a doublewide Haven-to-Heaven highway.

18.

The ocean at dawn. My jeans rolled to my bruised knees. The brittle snap of the sea. My bones, my teeth, my shivering skate key. I let my body soak in the freeze. Bent and washed my face. Watched the Band-Aid float away, the dark stain of blood where the skin had split. My shins, my hands turned another color.

There was no getting clean.

There was a couple down by the tide, big hats on, poking through the remnants of the storm. There were brothers or cousins, kids I'd never seen before, screaming after a bird. Far away, in the gentle break of the waves, that spotted deer stood. I could see the places where its hooves had poked into the sand and how its ears twitched, but when I turned to slosh out of the sea it ran, and now, down on South, someone hoisted a kite with a bedsheet tail.

First orange, first pink of the day.

I looked for the girl with the ladybug wings. I looked for Eva and the O'Sixteens. There were more people walking out of the haze, maybe strangers or maybe people I'd known before—Cammy Vaughn and Missy Ator and Nan Higgins, the knitting circle, the tenors from Community Arts—but I wasn't sure. They were far off, and I was walking now, drenched and cold, the sea in my hair, and the sky was more pink and more gold.

I'd left Old Carmen sleeping. I'd left Sterling guarding the walrus. I was walking.

Sometimes you hear things that aren't there. Sometimes you don't hear what is. I wasn't nearly sure of anything. Nothing was purely blue, and nothing was purely clear, and I didn't know, not anymore, what time it was, or what day.

When I heard the moan I thought it was either nothing or far out at sea. I was walking and the pink was turning gold and there was a breeze and inside the breeze was a sound or no sound, there, or not there, like that deer that maybe instead was a mirage. My body kept walking, but my mind said *Stop*. I cupped my hand to one ear like a conch shell. I waited for some kind of sign.

Nothing, or at least not at first. I stayed where I was, waiting on certain. I turned to the waves; they just kept coming. I turned in the direction of where the town used to be and where the mess still was. The sound wasn't far, and it was actual.

Very close, and very real.

"Hey," I said, and no one answered. Nothing again, and then a quiet *thwack*. I stood. I walked. I crept ever nearer. A McCauley's crate and something trapped inside. My pulse was in my throat.

Home of the brave, I thought. Whatever it was, however bad it was, this was pure and clear: the thing inside that crate needed me. I was the one it was depending on.

I was close enough now to peer through the slats. I held my own breath. Between the splintery wood, I saw a black thing go *thwack*. I saw a furry edge, and the color cinnamon.

"Hey," I said again. "Hey. Hey." Lifting the crate fast but still careful now. You can do this, I was thinking.

"Almost free," I was saying. "Gotcha, big fella." And now the crate was off and it was Cinnamon Nose right there, but only his tail was moving. I threw my arms around his neck. I kissed his whiskery, sandpaper nose. I said his name, over and over, Deni's name, too, told him how, forevermore, he'd be Deni's good-luck news. Now, pulling back, I saw what the trouble was—how the dog's back legs were tied up with burlap string, as if he'd stepped into a trap. I could see the places where the rope had cut in, slicing the skin, leaving him festered. I could see how hard it hurt. The knot was a Chinese puzzle, and now when I reached in to see what I could do about untying him, he yelped a terrible yelp, he begged me not to. I could see something like tears in his eyes. *Don't touch,* he was begging. *Please don't.*

He'd lost blood. He was trapped. He was so far from home. He tried to talk, but he couldn't, like his bark had been taken, too.

"We're going to fix you up," I promised. "No lie, Cinnamon Nose. Worst of this is done with now, you hear? I promise you."

He tried to stand but he couldn't. He tried to tell me something about his surviving—inside that crate, no water, no food, his legs lassoed. I couldn't tell how long he'd been there. I didn't know why he hadn't been found. I just knew that I had to get him to North and that the sand would take us, the crate would be his sled.

"You'll see," I said, and now I worked like hell— flipping the crate upright, shredding bedsheets that I found, making do with what we had.

You can do this, Mira Banul.

We can do this, Cinnamon Nose.

We set off for North. I pulled my special parcel true— over the sand, between the ruins. The bedsheets held. The crate didn't bust. The two of us were a spectacle, a small parade that became a bigger one as the people of dawn joined in, pushing from behind, clearing a path, helping me out with the load.

"Dog needs to get home" is all I said. And everyone on Haven understood.

19.

The sea had gnawed off most of North. Entire chunks of land were missing, and the houses with them, the docks, the boats, and it wasn't that the lighthouse had fallen, it was that the lighthouse was leaning, its stripes at an angle and its beacon blown off.

I rounded the bend of it. I saw Chang and Mario way up ahead. I saw Taneisha, her arm full of bracelets, and the houses ripped in half, the curtains blowing in empty rooms, somebody's attic on the ground, the backyard gardens in the street and a bird at a birdfeeder hung from a lampshade.

There was the buzz of insects and the rot of food and the carcasses of dead fish, and the brigade, at last, up ahead, and now Chang saw me, and she called out, and Deni came running, fast as Deni could run—her arm in that sling, her brother's boots on, the sky on the top of her head.

"Found him," I said. "Cinnamon Nose." And now the parade stepped back, it gave us room, I reached into the crate, I kissed that dog on the top of his very gorgeous head.

"Look who's here for you," I said, and Deni—Deni couldn't stop sobbing, couldn't stop thanking me, couldn't believe her good luck, because it was luck, she agreed, and it was also, she said, her dad and her brother looking down, and she hugged that dog, and at last he barked. He found a word or two, for Deni.

"He's hurt pretty bad," she finally said, through her tears.

"He needs some food," I said. "Some water."

"Yeah."

"He needs some help with his back legs."

"I see."

She pushed her hand through the spikes of her hair, rearranged her sunglasses. She patted her cheeks to dry her tears. She thought for a Deni minute, and she got herself a plan.

"Let's get him to the brigade," she said.

She stood beside me. Took the bedsheets in her hand. Halved the weight of the sled. She talked to that dog the entire time, listing out the what-nexts, making sure he understood.

20.

It was close to dusk by the time I returned to the rock, my clothes so full of dog hair and sweat salt that Sterling got suspicious in a second. She stayed away, though I talked to her. She pretended she couldn't hear. I gave up after a while and went down to the tide. I cleaned myself up. I watched the sunset. I sacrificed my blisters to the sea.

Sterling liked me better after that and even more after I traded my furry shirt for a cleaner hoodie, and when Old Carmen disappeared somewhere, I grabbed that cat and put her on my lap and told her she'd have been real proud of me and my rescue operation, that jealousy looks good on no one, that she was better than that. I said cats and dogs have to get along. I said, "So what did you make of yourself today?" and she looked at me with her sea-glass eyes, thinking maybe I was crazy.

I served up a can of salmon. I made myself some peanut butter–marshmallow crackers. I was famished, I realized, and my bones were starting to show, and there was hardly anything between the purple bruise above my heart and my heart itself. I touched my chest. I felt my ribs. I thought of Jasper Lee, so far away. The hospital. The dark. I remembered a winter night, long ago, when it was just me and Mickey and Jasper Lee, lying side by side on the deck—the tartan blanket across us, the patchwork quilt, a pile of winter jackets. It was that cold. It was that bright. We had followed Mickey's flashlight out onto the deck, and we had lain down and covered up, and we were together, the three of us, safe, no one and no disease could touch us. There were white dwarves above our heads and black holes and red giants, and nobody cared, even I didn't care, what the stars were called. We just cared about the astronomical gleam. We said that it, like all the sky, belonged only to us.

We were greedy that way, the Banuls. We were greedy in the ways we had to be.

"Found it," Jasper Lee said that night.

"Found what?" Mickey asked him.

"My star," he said. He took his little hand out from beneath the blankets and pointed, but we still couldn't tell which star was his—maybe his hand was too small, maybe the stars were too thick. Mickey strained to see, then sat up quick. Felt around for her flashlight, the old doublewide. She flipped the switch. She handed it over to my brother.

"Show us," she said, snuggling back down into the warmth with us.

Showing is what my little brother did. Six years old, and there he lay, shining his light on his favorite star, like the flashlight was the size of a Hollywood spotlight. He beamed the light up steady so that it was perfectly clear—his imperfect star, shining perfectly bright.

"Best star in the universe," he said, and we believed, and we lay like that, waiting for the sky to burst even brighter above us.

Now, dusk fallen, Old Carmen still gone, the people of the beach pulling up their bedding for a new night, and the gulls doing their bedtime screech, I felt around on that rock and found the doublewide and flipped that switch.

I pointed it in the direction of the mainland.

I stared along the yellow ridge into the dark.

"Best star in the universe," I whispered, to Jasper Lee.

And I waited, and I waited for him to whisper back.

21.

I woke early the next day. Sterling had stayed close, slept, snored tiny cat snores. She had, I knew, forgiven me. That's what we do in families.

I stretched until the ache eased from my muscles. I touched the purple place above my heart.

On her end of things Old Carmen was sharpening a knife on the face of the rock, making a nice percussion of sound. She looked up when I sat up. She said nothing for a while. She turned her head to watch the tide, the early people who were rising. Little kids running with sand in their hair. Parents shaking out blankets, rinsing out pots, unscribbling the piles they had slept with.

"You get that dog home proper?" Old Carmen asked.

"Yes, ma'am."

"That's some good work," she said. "Be proud of it."

I nodded. I was. We were quiet. We let the world wake up some more and then Old Carmen spoke again. "Time is running out," she said.

"What does the radio say?"

"The radio says 'patience.' We're going to need more than that, though. We're going to need provisions." It was like the saving of Mid was all on her shoulders. Like we'd voted her in charge, and maybe, somehow, we had. She looked beaten down a little, worn out, worried. She closed her eyes, put her chin on her fist, let the early sun fall against her million lines and wrinkles.

I looked south, toward the cottage, no parts of it visible in the early mist. I thought of the room high up on stilts, the note I'd left, the creepiness I'd felt. I thought of all I'd sheltered, too, and of how Mickey and Jasper Lee would want me to use it right, to share it now, to be that kind of greedy. And brave.

"Will you keep an eye on Sterling?" I asked Old Carmen now.

"Haven't lost that cat yet."

"Okay," I said. "All right. I'm going." I climbed down off the rock. Did one huge body stretch.

22.

Through the mist Rapunzel came into view, hanging like a long blond braid. Next came the stilts, the deck, the parts of the house that the wind was blowing through. The sand went from firmer to softer as I walked, and then, at last, I was there. I reached for the rope and it held fast. I climbed with blistered hands.

I hurtled myself over the edge of the deck. I turned and a dozen dolphins were out in the waves, slicing the rising sun with their fins. The scavengers and combers and cousins were distant, a gull leading them off on the chase. The fire rose from Old Carmen's rock, a quarter mile off.

On the deck the sand had blown into new ridges and cracks. Inside the attic the shadows were blue. The drawers I'd closed were open again. The path between the stacks of things seemed interrupted, somehow, disturbed, and I turned. There was someone on my bed.

Like the waves had rolled her in.

Like she hadn't heard me coming.

Someone. A girl.

I stepped back, held my breath, watched from the shadows. She had a face of vaguely foreign angles and a sleeve of tattoos, earrings that squiggled down her neck, bare feet, chipped nails. She was lying on her side, my mother's patchwork quilt pushed to one side, and she was dressed in the things she'd stolen: my aunt's Marilyn Monroe T-shirt, her faux tuxedo jacket, the long red skirt I'd worn one Halloween. "What are you?" Deni had kept asking that year. "A gypsy," I kept saying, though she wouldn't believe me until we'd gone all the way to her house and she'd found me a pair of gold hoops and also a Rothko bandanna to tie on my head, because somehow the Rothko was gypsy. It was that skirt, the gypsy skirt, that the stranger had on, and below the hem of that skirt, on those dark, bare feet, were three of my aunt's fake-crystal toe rings, taken from the drawer. I heard a scuffle on the floor and looked down. By the bed was a bright orange cage, the size of a clutch, and inside that cage was a painted hermit crab, the prettiest crab I'd ever seen, tiptoeing back and forth, waving one claw like a sign.

There was a broom. I reached for it. Held it like a weapon. Heard Deni in my ear: *Defenses.*

"Hey."

She didn't open an eye. She didn't stir. It was like she'd come, gone shopping, decided to stay—an overgrown

Goldilocks with the darkly tanned skin, her eyelids like two dark hoods, her fingers twined into her fingers, like she was hiding something. I leaned across her, broom still high, pulled my mother's quilt away, threw it over my own shivering shoulders, because right is right, she could not take that from me. Even in this bizarre fairy tale we were living.

"Hey," I said again.

She sighed. Straightened one leg. The gold on her toes flashed with the sun. The rest of her was quiet.

I touched her shoulder now, the tip of the broom to the seam of the Marilyn tee, the place beneath the squiggle of her earring. I nudged, pushed harder, wondered, for a moment, if she was dead, but she sighed again, and now she opened her eyes, and her eyes were like seaweed, caught in a dream, in the haze. Eyes without a trace of shame.

"I knocked," she said. "Nobody answered."

I tried to picture that—this girl, she seemed my age, climbing the rope, crossing the deck, knocking on—what? The open sliding door? The shadows? I pictured her looking around and deciding to stay, because of course she'd been there before, the hours ahead of the storm, and later, leaving her footprints through the narrow path from the bed to the room's two doors. She'd been here before, it had to be her, and she'd knocked? She'd looked around and stayed? Helped herself to the clothes she found? Brought along a crab in a cage? I pictured her coming and going, searching and staying, placing her crab by my bed. She wasn't just some girl. She had come before. She had a reason.

"Nobody was home," she said.

There were puckered places beneath each eye, like she'd been crying. There were shadows on her ankles, but when she moved, they moved with her. Bruises, I realized. Hurt, like the rest of us.

"Who are you?"

She shook her head.

"What's your name?"

"Gillian." Her words were sleepy, slow.

"You've been here before. You keep coming back. What do you want?"

She looked up at me. She was good with a lie, seemed to be; that's how I read her.

"Dusk before the storm," I said. "Hours before it got crazy. You were here."

She shook her head no. "Wasn't me."

"What's your last name, Gillian?"

She shrugged.

"Why are you lying to me?"

"I'm not."

"If you were from here, I would know you, but I don't know you. What do you want?"

She looked away from me like I had hurt her. Like I was the one who had trespassed here, like who she was and why she'd come were none of my business. "Look around," she said, after a while. "Everyone's a refugee. No one belongs anywhere, not anymore."

"This is my house, and I don't trust you."

Still the broom between us. Still the girl lying to me.

Beyond the room and the deck, the sky was blue and clouds were puffing in, and in the sea the dolphins had disappeared, but the giraffe was riding in with the tide. I heard her breathe three times, like yoga breaths. I heard her start to talk, but it was hard, at first, to find any sense in the story she told. She was from far away—that is what she said. Had moved to Haven in July and stayed, a castaway, that's what she said. Johnny Carpenter, she said. Did I know him? Down by the trailer park?

That park being gone, she said. Johnny being gone. Did I know it? Did I know him? That's where she'd come from.

"I don't know a Johnny Carpenter," I said.

"He lived in the park," she said. "Like I did."

Afternoon of the storm, she said, Johnny went out. *Be right back,* he'd said, but he didn't come back, and then the night came in, and then the storm came in, and her name was Gillian, and she'd been up and down the beach looking for Johnny, calling his name, until it was time gone by, and she was cold and wet, and when she saw the rope, she climbed it.

"That is all," she said. "Sorry. End of story."

"Rapunzel," I said.

"Rapunzel?" She shook her head.

"Name of the rope."

There was sand in her hair. There were bruises on her ankles.

"Nobody was home," she repeated.

"Not exactly the safest domicile," I said.

She'd knocked. She'd called out. She'd gone downstairs. Tried to, but the stairs had melted, did I know that, and there were fish down there on the floor—dead fish and seaweed, a TV flat on its back, a carton of eggs; that was the smell, or part of it. Nobody home, and so she came back upstairs, and she was so tired, she said, that she had found the quilt and slept.

"Start at the beginning," I said. "The afternoon before the storm. What is your story for then?"

"I don't know what you're talking about," she said, and she began to shiver, and if Mickey had been home, if the place were still a home, she'd have brought this girl tea, and if Jasper Lee had been near he'd have shown her sand, and if Eva had been found, she'd be sitting on my bed, holding Gillian's hand, and if Deni were with me, she'd have said, *We've got a brigade up at North. Room enough. Food.*

"What was your plan?" I said.

"I was tired," she repeated. "I'm not staying, am I?"

She said it like a question. Hung it on the line between us. I heard the waves, the slap of the surf. I listened to her breathing. She was a refugee like the rest of us. A minor thief, but maybe not a liar. She was just a girl, maybe not much older than me. She had been looking for Johnny. She had bare feet, no boots. She had a crab in a cage like a purse. I was losing track of who had come, and how often. Of what had been said, and what was true.

She sat and I stood. She moved and I didn't. I asked her what she knew about Mid Beach and she said nothing at all. "This is as far as I got," she said, "looking for Johnny." I said a quarter mile up there was a rock and a fire and Old Carmen, a working radio.

"Radio?"

"Battery-operated. Gets the news."

"What's the news?" she said.

"Big storm. No bridge. Patience."

"Patience?" she said. *"Patience?"*

"Haven is on its own," I said. "For a while. That's the news."

She started to cry. Big tears on wide cheeks. She put her hands on her face and her tattoos swirled up her wrist and disappeared into that shirt and ended just below her chin.

"I don't know anybody," she said. "Just Johnny, and I can't find him. The whole place blew. It's all on its side down there. I can't find Johnny."

Sometimes you have to decide. I decided. Sometimes you don't know, so you tell yourself you do; you choose. I chose to believe that she was who she said she was—a

Gillian looking for a Johnny. I lay down the broom. I crossed the narrow channel of the room. I sat with her. I took her hand in mine.

"Nobody even knows I'm here," she said. "I'm no one without Johnny."

"Do you cook?" I asked, after a while.

She sniffed. "A little."

"Can you fish?"

"Johnny taught me. I'm not so bad at it, when the fish come around."

"Okay," I said. "Then it's decided."

I pulled a new shirt from the closet, a new sweater, new jeans, and changed. I reached for bags that hung from the hooks in my aunt's closet, reached for the shirts, the skirts, the pants, the robes this woman I had never met once wore. There were three canvas bags and a wheely suitcase. I found them. I stuffed them. I'd decided, and it was like Gillian knew what to do, where things were, how to pack endless stuff into three bags and a suitcase, how she could help.

This? she'd ask.

This, too?

She told me the name of her crab: Sarah. Why Sarah? It's a pretty name. It fits her. Asked had I seen the deer on the beach, and I told her that I had, and had I seen a kite, or was that smoke. If it was South it was a kite, I said, if it was Mid it was smoke, Old Carmen's smoke, and yes, there was a girl in glitter wings; I had seen her, too. Into three canvas bags and one wheely suitcase we packed—my aunt's clothes, her binoculars, the patchwork quilt, a pair of knives, filleting tools—anything that could help the people of Mid, anything that could answer Old Carmen's call, until at last there was nothing more to pack and Gillian changed into a pair of jeans and a shirt that my aunt must have worn twenty years ago. They fit her like a glove.

"What's next?" Gillian asked.

"We toss it," I say. "We haul it to the people at Mid."

"Toss it? Like grenades?"

"Like grenades. I'll show you."

I dragged an overstuffed bag down the thin alley between things, over the sliding-door threshold, down the slope of the deck, to the rail. I hollered out and I tossed the thing and it went bomb-blasting down.

"All right," she said, as if she had to think about this. She dragged a bag of her own through the banks of sand to the edge of the deck, hoisted it above the rail, threw it down. A minor bomb blast. Two more tosses and we'd be out of there, but now in the corner of my eye, I saw another paper bird lift off in the breeze and float. Gillian turned in a mega instant and reached. I reached first. Grabbed the paper bird and unfolded its wing. Stared down at the page.

Tell me who you are, and what you're taking.

Those were my words.

What belongs to me.

Those were not.

I looked at her. I squinted hard.

"What?" she said.

"What's this?" I asked.

I stood in the lamp of the sun and read again. My words and the other ones, in spidery blue-green.

"I trusted you," I said.

"You can trust me."

"Show me how you write," I said.

"How I *write*?"

"Yeah. Write. Don't move." I trudged back through the sand, reached for a pen that I'd tucked into a housecoat pocket, turned the paper over and handed her the ink, like ink was a weapon.

"Write your name," I said.

"You have to trust me," she said.

"I need proof."

"I've told you who I am."

We stared at each other, the longest time. A ray of sun got in my eye. I tried to think or to somehow reason. She was a castaway looking for a boy she'd lost. She'd climbed Rapunzel and found a bed and slept. She was who she said she was, or else she wasn't.

What belongs to me.

Own the words, Gillian. But she wouldn't.

"There are libraries on the beach," she said. "Leashes are empty. A Honda Civic is parked into the tide. What isn't strange anymore?"

She was just a girl, and the storm had changed us. She had nothing. That was her story. She had written words she wouldn't confess to, or maybe she hadn't, and I had to stand there and decide.

"Come on," I finally said.

She hooked the purse of the hermit crab cage over one wrist. Went down first, hand over hand.

I watched the part in the dark of her hair.

23.

It was Deni up ahead. Deni, who'd been waiting for me at the rock and had started running as soon as she'd seen me, then pulled up short when she realized that the tall girl in the borrowed getup wasn't just near me but with me. The glasses on Deni's head reflected the Brillo Pad clouds. She'd traded her brother's sweatshirt for a nubby pink turtleneck her mother used to wear on Sundays. Her combat boots were dark with ocean and mud. She extended her good hand like the minister's daughter she was. She had something to tell me about Cinnamon Nose; I knew it. She had news of another kind as well, and it wasn't news for strangers.

"Deni," she said.

"Gillian," Gillian answered.

"I found her," I said. "In my room."

Deni's eyebrow arched high. She was beside me as we walked toward the rock, Gillian just a little behind and the key around my neck beating the bruise. A toaster. A chaise lounge. The spinning wheel Darlene kept in the front of her house. The music stand that Mr. Friedley used for important all-school occasions. The green awning that Cammy Vaughn rolled out each spring, so that she could sit and test the inaugural mint juleps of her crowd. The bird-bath that had sat outside the How to Live store for as long as I could remember.

The things on the beach weren't only things.

They had once been somethings to someones.

Deni had something to say, and even then, after that storm, some things were private.

I glanced over my shoulder. Gillian walked, her eyes cast down. She was cautious among all the shards and splinters.

At the rock Old Carmen looked up, shielded her eyes from the sun, took a long, startled look at Gillian—a head-to-toe look, saying nothing. She looked at Deni and she looked at me and then she stood up and rearranged the rock so that the castaway would have a place on it. Just like that. Special privileges for a girl who'd shown up in my bed. Like Old Carmen had done for me, she was doing for the girl. Deni got that look on her face. The kind that said, *Whoa. Hold on. Be careful.*

"Gillian," I said, furthering the introductions. "She fishes."

"That right?"

"Yes, ma'am. So she says."

"You a fisherwoman, Gillian?" Old Carmen asked.

Gillian shivered. She nodded. Deni rocked back and forth in her ocean-squeaky boots. She crossed her arms across her chest, barely holding on to her news now, hardly polite anymore, eager for us to get away. Just the two of us. The bright sun of morning had not yet returned. We were little people under a gray-blue Brillo Pad. I told Old Carmen I had business with Deni, and Sterling, pacing the edge of the rock, took an all-flying leap into my arms and licked my cheek with her sandpaper tongue.

"Hey," I said. "What did I tell you, Sterling? Jealous looks good on no one."

I gave Sterling a kiss between the ears, ran my hand across her back, over her tail. I whispered truths into her ear. I said my best friend Deni needed me.

She settled back quick. I gave Gillian a look. I told Old Carmen I'd be back as soon as I could and she said:

"No shenanigans."

We left Old Carmen there, by the beach with Gillian, Sterling in charge of them both.

24.

"It's Eva," Deni said. "Eva's been found."

"Tell me. Everything."

But it was hard for Deni to start, hard for her to get the sequence right, and now she was running, and I was, too, following behind in her footsteps, catching the words that flew.

"She's not dead," she said.

"Okay," I said. "Okay." Breathing out. *She's not dead.* The story's only good part. The clouds seemed to be dropping to earth. The waves and the gulls were crashing, too. The sand was squish. We ran.

"Slow down," I told Deni, but now her story came out in a rush, pieces of it out of order, erased and replaced and starting over. Eva had been found out at the lighthouse beneath a ripped-from-its-own-bolts bench. Unconscious. Broken. The bones in both legs snapped. The twins, Deni was saying. Becca and Deby, who had gone out in the night.

Said they couldn't sleep. Maybe they were scavenging, Deni didn't know. They were the ones who'd found Eva. Thought she was just some pile of clothes at first, but then there was Eva's hair. Glowing gold.

Deni herself, she hadn't been sleeping. She had been lying there in the dark and then she heard those jingle bells that Becca wears and she stood up and went to the window and knew. Saw Becca running. Heard Becca calling. Turned around and said, "It's Eva," and everyone was on their feet in minutes, up in the dark—out of their broken houses and into the dark and some of them rushing to the lighthouse, running behind Becca, leading the way with her jingle bells, toward Eva, Deby, the lighthouse. Some of them getting ready to triage on a porch.

"Eva's not dead," I said.

"No," Deni huffed. "She's not."

But Eva wasn't talking, either, not opening her eyes, and what she needed, Deni said, was the mainland hospital, where Jasper Lee and Mickey were—a broken bridge and two hours away and nobody knew, besides, how the hospital had fared in the storm. Eva needed care and she had the brigade but that wasn't enough. No X-rays. No anesthesia. No sterile environment. Hardly enough clean water. Two nurses and a doctor and the First Aid and Rescue instructor, Rosie's sister, who had taught us counting with blue Slurpees.

My stomach sickened. I couldn't catch my breath. I wanted to stop and cry, but Deni was all-out running now, the clouds on her head, and I was running, too. We had a long way to go. Eva wasn't dead.

"One more thing," Deni said, calling back to me, the gap between us lengthening, and I needed my skates more than anything. I needed a straight stretch of asphalt.

"Yeah?"

"She was wearing Shift's hoodie. She had her binoculars back."

"What?"

"We have to hurry."

I couldn't hurry any faster than that.

25.

Like an open-air camp. Like a Civil War scene. Like *M*A*S*H*, the TV show Mickey would watch in late-night reruns, when, after four jobs and us, she still couldn't sleep. I didn't know the nurses or the doctor, but I knew Rosie's sister, Andra— her long blond hair up in a ponytail and her eyes so blue and her hands busy unwinding and rewinding gauze, as if she didn't know what else she could do.

Chang and Mario and Taneisha were there, like a mirage. Becca with her jingle bells and Deby, with her eyes behind her bangs, and Ginger, who had lost her tiara and the orange burnish of her hair. It was some kind of miracle, lost and found, the O'Sixteens reconstituted, who knows how. They'd found the warped plane of a dining room table that still had two of its legs. They'd set the legless end down on the shoulders of a La-Z-Boy chair and wedged some roof shingles beneath the table legs to help the horizontal—all under the guidance of Deni, I'd find out later. Deni, who always knew what she could do. By the time I arrived, Deni had cleared away room, asking Becca and Ginger to step aside, so that I could get up close to Eva, hold her right hand, which weighed nothing, as if the sea had leached her bones. Then Taneisha stepped away from the other side and gave Deni Eva's other hand and we both stood there, breathing hard and out of breath and looking down at our best friend.

Don't let go, I thought. Eva. We're here.

"We're hoping she can hear you," someone said, and I looked up and there was Dr. Edwards. His beard had gone shaggy. His bangs were in his eyes. The dark part of his hair had turned a sudden white. He had on somebody's Christmas snowman sweater and his neck seemed swollen, his Adam's apple huge, as if he hadn't swallowed once since the monster blew. I thought of class, a lifetime ago: *I believed that I was perishing with the world, and the world with me.*

But that guy, whoever he was, had not perished, and Eva had not perished, either, and now, when I looked away, past Eva, across Deni's shoulder, I saw Cinnamon Nose in the corner of the porch, his legs cut free of the rope and wrapped in gauze, his snout down on his paws.

"Eva," I said. "We were looking everywhere."

I tried to play back what I knew, put the story together, figure out just what had happened here. Eva had gone out with Shift. She was found in his hoodie. Her binoculars were there, around her neck. They had gone to the lighthouse, and she'd been found alone, and where the hell was Shift?

Eva, beautiful Eva, heart-too-big-for-the-world Eva. It was as if a shadow had crept in under her skin—all those worlds she saw that none of us could see all stacked up high and dangerous inside her. Her eyes seemed stung—two purple welts, thin broken lashes. There was seaweed stitched into her curls, the broken leg of a starfish, the bones of fish. They'd drawn a sheet up to her chin, and I was glad, for I couldn't bear to imagine her legs.

"Eva," I said. "Wake up."

I looked up and there was Dascher, now, with her anchor healed. There was Tiny Tina blocking the sun that was starting to climb above the clouds, and there was Becca beside Deby, the two unalike twins who, standing side by side after the night they'd had, looked suddenly like sisters. Straight across from me Deni stood, Eva's hand in hers, her dog behind her, a big tear rolling down her cheek. None of us on Haven could afford to lose another thing.

"We're all here, Eva," I said, and maybe I imagined it, maybe you will say that I did, but I felt a tremor in my hand and I believed that it was coming from her, and now, when I looked up again, I saw Deni untangling the curls of Eva's hair. I saw Taneisha and Tiny Tina at the opposite end, rubbing the soles of Eva's feet, the decals all gone from her toenails. Hung from a makeshift post, I saw that hoodie and those pink binoculars.

Down the street, I saw the blown-apart living room of some poor person's home—only two walls up, the floral wallpaper dripping. I saw people dressed in February clothes and garden gloves, a working unity. It was the food brigade, I realized, turning its attention to the meal of the day, to the cartons of things taken from McCauley's, the cans of things that had rolled around, then back, with the tide, the things they could do to make a difference.

I thought of Old Carmen down at Mid, and her own brigade. I thought of Gillian, who said she could fish, the fake-crystal toe rings on her bare feet, no boots, her crab bright as a clown fish. I thought of Sterling, patient and respectful and learning not to be jealous. I thought of Mickey and Jasper Lee and the bridge of light between us.

Only thing not replaceable is people. Order. Family. Genus. Species. We were the kingdom unto Haven.

I leaned down again to kiss Eva's pale forehead. I combed a fishbone from her curls with my fingers. I looked over my shoulder at Dr. Edwards and Andra and all those whose names I didn't know, who were hovering near, who had done what they could—cleaned the wounds, set the bones beneath the sheet, made Eva comfortable.

"Wake up, Eva," I whispered again. "We're all here."

PART *Three*

l.

There were four of us on the rock that night. From up above we might have looked like the starfish that had left one tip inside Eva's hair. From below we looked like the lucky ones. The extra sweaters, towels, and sheets I'd hauled from home had gone only so far—Old Carmen handing them out earlier in the day to whoever needed them most. That's what she had said, just a few words, when I'd returned, late, from North. I'd stayed until dusk fell, until Dr. Edwards said that it was time to let Eva rest, even though all she had done that day was rest and rest, listen to the stories we told her, the cities we found, *Wake up, Eva. Wake up.* Her heart beating and her lungs breathing but her thoughts so very far away, all those layers that she kept inside, the past and the eternal, a coma or a dream. We didn't know. We needed help. A hospital.

Gillian's earrings ran like black tears down her neck. She sat on the rock wearing one of my aunt's old sweaters like a cape and a pair of damp, ribbed socks on her feet.

It was cold. The heavy clouds had returned. Some-one began to cry, and kept on crying, the saddest sound, and I sat up, found my doublewide, shined its light on the huddles, the blankets, the sheets, the awning canvases, the umbrella fabric under and over which the beach people slept, but the crying stopped, as if the light had shamed it, and now someone began playing that stuck song on the piano and someone tapped up the beat on the Maytag and Old Carmen snored through it and Gillian lay silent, not saying a word. Gillian, the castaway, on Old Carmen's rock.

Up at North, Deni and the brigade were taking care.

"I'm coming back," I said. "I promise." To Eva. To Deni. To Cinnamon Nose and the brigade. To Dr. Edwards, who had found James Joyce in the wreckage and was reading it out loud. I left him holding our best friend's hand:

"'Once upon a time and a very good time it
was there was a moocow coming down along
the road and this moocow that was coming down
along the road met a nicens little boy named
baby tuckoo. . . .'"

"Don't let anything happen to Eva," I'd said.
"We're all right here," the others said.

"Hey," Deni said, just before I started back. She put out her hand, the one still caught in the sling. She asked for mine. There, on my palm, lay her brother's glory medals.

"He's giving you his strength," she said.

2.

I woke to drops of rain near the edge of dawn. I woke to the
sound of Old Carmen's snores and to the silent sleeping of
the girl on the rock, Gillian, who had stolen in and stayed,
whose story sounded strange—a lie or the truth, I didn't
know. She'd been given a place with us: Old Carmen's
choice; Old Carmen making room.

I pulled the trench coat over my head, held it up, like
a tent.

"Here, Sterling," I said.

That cat, nesting in.

I slept.

I slept again.

3.

I dreamed or I did not.

Mickey was near, and she was not.

She had news, or there was silence.

I slept, or I dreamed, or I did not, and now I was remembering something from long ago, my mother's words: *I don't know what to do.*

What was I? Nine? What was my brother? What was Mickey? I never knew—her birthday slipping by each year without candles, without any kind of cake. I was dreaming or remembering, and there we were in the ghost of the cottage, on the second floor of that attic that was newly my room, though the life my aunt had left behind would always be bigger than the life I'd live, her things more present than mine, those closets full of her empty skirts and sleeves, her cracked-sole shoes, her straw hats, some of them with strands of hair inside. I was nine, and Mickey was crying, and we were side by side on the bed my aunt had left behind, and Jasper Lee was downstairs, Jasper Lee and his missing iduronate-2-sulfatase, his diagnosis. That was the news.

"It isn't fair," Mickey was saying. Words thick between tears. "My son. His whole life. A goddamned enzyme."

She took my hand and squeezed. She lifted my chin with her other palm. She shook her head no, and the tears fell again.

I was nine—that's right—and my mother was near, on the bed beside me, with her impossible news.

The sea was beyond us, gray and green. The rise and the crash and the colors and all those monsters. I could see the sea through the window, past the deck, across the sand. On top of the curio cabinet, in a silver frame, I saw the face of Mickey's sister, my aunt with her glamorous hair and her eyes stealing away from the camera snap, already gone. Mickey reached for the frame. She held the photo on her lap. She let the sea do its business on the shore.

"I always longed for a sister," she said. "Someone to talk to."

"You have a sister," I said.

"Not a real one," Mickey said. "Not someone I can talk to."

"Maybe she's different now," I remember saying. "Maybe she would talk if you called."

"No." That's all my mother said. "No." The definitive answer.

I woke, and it was dawn. There was the flapping of the No Surrender flag above our heads. There was the patch-work quilt on the place of that rock where Old Carmen had spent the night snoring. She was down by the shore now, up to her knees, in the tide, the line of her fishing rod casting way, way out.

The fire was low.

The rain had stopped.

Sterling and Gillian slept.

I walked down the rock stairs toward her.

4.

Maybe I'm medium everything, but beside Old Carmen I was tall. I smelled like the days that had passed, the dreams I had had, and my teeth and my tongue were peach fuzz. My jeans were rolled to my knees, stiff as cardboard. My underwear was gross. My many layers were like many arms. My hair was clouds.

Old Carmen had stripped to her flannel shirt. She'd never changed her pants, and in her face were the first pokes of sun, and the hook at the end of her line was catching nothing but some of the things the storm had run off with. One half of a pair of green tube socks. The zebra wrap of someone's phone. A package of seeds no one had planted. A bright pink disk, like the sun.

"Chang's Frisbee," I said as she reeled it in.

She unhooked it with one gesture.

She shook it dry.

She slid it toward me and cast again.

We stood there, side by side.

The giraffe from the Mini Amuse was bobbing on the horizon, nicking the beginning of the sun. Alice in Wonderland had sailed to Atlantis. The tide was sucking hard, urging us forward, crinkling our knees, sinking our feet deeper in. I leaned down, troweled into the sand with the Frisbee and tilted it toward the sun. I thought of all the ways that sand had been made, each speck the end of something that had lived and died and crumbled. *Crumble.* It would have been the name of Jasper Lee's Project Flow, had everything that happened never happened.

The dolphins were in the near beyond, their fins slicing the waves, easy, easy. They had come from the south. They were headed toward North. They began to swim a circle right before us. There are forty species of dolphins. They come in black and white and pink and gray; they are the size of dogs or the size of cabooses. They swim the rivers and the seas, they dream in every language, they find their way through the music they make, they know if you are pregnant. *The dolphin is the heart of the sea,* I'd written for my Project Flow, seemed like forever ago. *In many tales, in much of science, the dolphin is the savior.*

Between the human and the shark, it has swum circles of protection.

Beneath the drowning girl, the drowning boy, the drowning ship, it has risen, it has buoyed, it has rafted.

Toward the fisherman's pole it has sent the brightest fish, along the banks of some beaches it has harvested its dinners, in the deep of the sea, it has made its own kind of love, and it has played, and it is this love and this play that makes dolphins almost human.

Apollo was a dolphin once.

Aphrodite rode a dolphin's back.

Dionysus turned a band of pirates into slick and silvery dolphins. He set them free.

And, once, in a fresco painted thirty-five hundred years ago, dolphins and deer were the "great leaping" things. They were the best beauty man had ever seen.

Project Flow. I will finish it someday. I will finish it for you, Ms. Isabel.

Old Carmen and I stood watching the silver fins slice, the bottlenosed snouts, the sun still rising. There was so much to say and so much to ask and so we were silent, saying nothing. She'd reel in, reel out, relieve her hook of its vagabond collection. I'd stand there with her bucket in one hand, waiting to stock up the community pantry.

"Have you heard the story," Old Carmen finally asked, "of Pelorus Jack?"

"No," I said. I hadn't.

"Pelorus Jack," she said. "The dolphin. Years 1888 through 1912. Guided ships traveling the strait between Wellington and Nelson. Waited for them. Led the way. Led them again on the way back. Pelorus Jack," she said. "Mark Twain traveled all that way to see him for himself."

"For real?" I said.

"It's history," she said.

Not a myth. Not a dream. Not a memory.

We stood there, and the dolphins came nearer. We stood there, and they circled closer again, and now Old Carmen began to sing a song from a long time ago, words by P. Cole, she said, music by H. Rivers, a song like a lullaby, not the words, maybe, but the way she sang it, gentle and understanding and slow.

"A famous fish there used to be, called Pelorus Jack
He'd always swim far out to sea, when a ship
came back
About her bow he'd dive and play,
And keep with her right to the bay
And all on board would cheer and say:
'There's Pelorus Jack.'

Pelorus, Pelorus, good Pelorus Jack
Pelorus, Pelorus, brave Pelorus Jack
Everyone cheered whenever he appeared
Pelorus, Pelorus, good Pelorus Jack.

For years he'd meet the ships like this,
good Pelorus Jack
It seemed as though he'd never miss, any

vessel's track
He surely was a jolly sort, and everybody as
they ought
Declared he was a real old sport; Good
Pelorus Jack.

One day a ship came home again, poor
Pelorus Jack
The people looked, but looked in vain, for his
shining back
And now as day goes after day, the folks all sigh
in mournful way
'Old Jack is gone,' they sadly say; Poor
Pelorus Jack."

Shhhhh, shhhhh, shhhhh. Her voice sounded like that. It sounded like the waves at night. It sounded like going under, going in. She sang the whole song, the whole silly song, and I closed my eyes not against it, but within it, and the tide was coming in and my feet were sinking deeper, and in the crumble of the sand I remembered that song, where I had heard it before, the faraway place of a night back then, the night when I was drowning. I felt myself going under. I felt myself buoyed up. I felt two hands beneath my head, heard someone singing. This was the song that had saved me. Hers were the hands. Hers were the feet in the sand.

Old Carmen.

"You were there," I said. "Weren't you? Back then?"

She lifted her shoulders.

She let them fall. Maybe she confessed.

She stuffed the rod between her knees. She touched my hand. "Look," she said. Because the dolphins were even closer now. Because if I reached out I could touch them. Because if I had asked, they'd have lent me their fins—to the sun and back, from here to Main, and also back again.

Safe passage home.

5.

The sun was full and gold by the time we left the sea. The people on the beach were rising, stretching, shaking off the night and the ruins of Haven. There was a single fish in Old Carmen's bucket—an early striped bass, *Morone saxatilis,* its dorsal fin like Viking sails, its olive skin fading to silver fading to white, its stripes like paper. Old Carmen did the humane thing. She would sizzle it later over the fire.

Sterling was walking the perimeter of the rock, like the good guard dog she'd become. Circling Eva's pink-bowed cactus, Old Carmen's black box with its infinite drawers, the radio with its battery power, the smoking embers. She leapt into my arms when I came near. She purred, and I heard her words. *Gillian is gone.* Her dark hair, her long earrings, the wrap of that tattoo, my aunt's fake crystals, the hermit crab in the Day-Glo cage.

Gillian was gone.

Sterling said so.

Those footsteps in the sand.

I needed fresh socks for the damp Skechers I'd been wearing since the storm. I needed to rub the salt crust from my legs. I needed to be ready for whatever would be next, Deni-style, and so I dug deep into the canvas bag Gillian had packed. Replenishments, I thought. Damn her, I thought. My hand knocked against something solid and smooth. Something wood, I realized, and glass.

Something stolen.

I pulled it out, and there it was—the face of my aunt in the frame she had left, a crack in the glass, the thing Gillian had come for. *The story of you,* I thought.

I thought of how well my aunt's clothes had fit the castaway. I thought of the crystal toe rings. I thought of the footprints, the words: *What belongs to me.* I thought of Gillian at ease in the bed, and how she wouldn't say her last name, refused to. I thought of everything a storm blows in and takes away and how we fight so hard through each reclaiming. I thought and then I felt a shadow. Old Carmen, on the rocks, watching me.

"Go," she said, "and find her."

I wouldn't have believed I could run anymore, and yet: I could have gone end to end, even Mode-less.

6.

I found her on my bed, I found her crying. Photos tossed like a quilt around her, the crab in its cage on the pillow, the whole place more damp and crooked and dangerous than it had ever been. It would all slide away soon, give up its ghosts, fall on its knees, crumble, but Gillian didn't care. Not about the danger and not that I was there. She didn't defend herself or argue.

"Who are you?" I asked at last.

"Gillian," she said, from a sobbing place. "Gillian. I told you."

She looked at the bed, I looked at the bed, the sea of pictures. They were gray and white and faded colors. They had scalloped edges, curled-in faces, shining places that had rubbed down dull, black ears on some of the corners. The pictures were Haven, Main on Haven, Uncle Willy's and Malarky's Pub and another version of How to Live and the Beachcomber with fake palm trees, and the beach itself, wider than I'd ever seen, the rocks in the right places, the cottage without its window boxes. They were two girls playing in ruffled bikinis, on a picnic bench, on a pleather trunk, in the sparkle of two pairs of wings. Two girls playing, and a bucket in one's hand, and a fishing pole with a little blowfish dangling. Two girls in every picture. Every single one.

"Gillian?" I said.

"My mother." She pointed to one girl.

"Your mother." She pointed to the other.

She showed me again.

Her mother. My mother.

My aunt. My Mickey.

In picture after picture, there they were.

"My mother's dead," she said.

I couldn't answer. Could not say one word. Reached for Gillian's hand. Held it. The only words I had.

"All the stories she told, when I was a kid, were of this beach," Gillian was saying, her voice soft, a whisper. "This house. This sea. This attic. Everything she loved was Haven. She'd left everything behind, she said. She hid her photos behind that panel," and now Gillian pointed to a broken place in the broken wall, a secret cove I'd not noticed before within the messy ruin. The wall was torn open and the space behind it was empty. All the photos my aunt had hidden in that secret cove were spread across the bed. "She told me where," Gillian said. "The last thing she said. Before she passed away."

What belongs to me, I thought.

What belongs. A note I was only meant to find if I hadn't discovered Gillian herself, asleep in my bed, covered by a blanket of sand. The words of an interrupted confessor.

I was desperate to understand; I couldn't. I understood only enough to try to imagine. Mickey's sister, the one who went away. Mickey's loss, before we had the science on Jasper Lee. She was my vanished aunt and Gillian's mother and these were the childhood stories Gillian needed, the proof she wanted of her mother's history, and now I thought of how I'd lived all these years with my mother's truest history stashed behind a wall beside my bed. How my mother lived with it *just this close.* Nothing was what it had been, but it *had* been. We were all castaways, looking for a part of the big confusing kingdom to call our very own, and to protect. There are no true words for how I felt right then. No words that I could tell you.

"So it was you," I said at last. "The day of the storm. Before it got crazy. It was you down there in the dusk."

Gillian shook her head, slow. She bit her lip. "No." She sat straight up. She turned toward me.

"It was Johnny," she said. "Johnny, looking for memories of our mom. My brother."

"Your *brother*?"

"Twins," she said. "Night and day, my mother called us. Nothing the same about us, except for the day we were born and the stories our mother told. Stories about this place. Stories from exile. That's what she said."

"Exile."

"How she called it."

"*Exile.* Jesus. Gillian. I'm sorry."

"I'm your half sister," she said. "Johnny's your half brother."

And now I was shaking my head, stuck on the word, *half.* On the idea of steps and partials. Half. I couldn't get the word to fit. I couldn't keep up with how fast the world kept changing.

"Your mom and my mom," she said. "Don't you see? Best friends. Best friends and perfect sisters, until this shit came around, this Vacationeer, my mom called him, this guy who loved them both, or acted like he did, left them pregnant, weeks apart. Your mom was the angry one. My mom was the one who left. They never spoke again to one another. But my mom—she was always talking about Haven. Calling it one *e* shy of Heaven. Saying to find out for myself. To find my mom's one sister. To find you. When she was dying, that's what she said. *Go find your family.* Mira, I had to."

"We're sisters?" I said.

"Half sisters," she said.

"I have another brother?"

"Half."

She made room for me on the bed. I crumpled beside her. She showed me pictures, one by one, and I told her the side of the stories I knew, the way I'd imagined it was. I thought of the bigness of Mickey's heart and the bigness of this sorrow, and how anger ruins everything, and how much chance in life is lost.

"My mom missed your mom," I said. "I know she did."

"My mom missed your mom. Always."

"I wish—"

"Yeah," Gillian said. "Me, too."

And then we were there with the breeze twirling in, looking for the past inside the pictures. We were looking back at the glamorous sisters in The Isolates' world. Carving their names inside picnic tables. Ordering Slurpees. Looking for swans. Promising Springsteen.

"So you weren't lying?" I said, finally.

"I wasn't lying."

"But."

"Johnny," she said, anticipating my next thing, the question she'd never really answered, the part of the puzzle that still didn't fit. "It was Johnny who had come to your house before the storm blew in. He was scouting for a way up and in."

"How do you know? For sure?"

"Because he told me his plan, because he was always full of plans—always doing things I'd never have done. We came to the island and I watched the sea, walked down here sometimes just to look up at you, see your mom and your brother, your friends on the beach, the deck where my mom would have been. Came and watched and walked away because you were here and this belonged to you and I couldn't figure out a way in. But Johnny—he wasn't afraid. He never was. We came and he became a part of Haven. Night and day, like my mother said. That day Johnny was going out, and he was saying he'd be back, and then the storm blew in. And—"

She covered her face with her hands.

"I know," I said, "I know," tears up and through me, too, because some things you can finally understand.

7.

A storm is the universe speaking. A storm is science. A storm takes everything away. Batters the rooftops, crashes the windows, tears up the gardens, sends the stop signs spinning. The walls are gone, the giraffe floats out to sea, the fawn shows up in the mist of dawn, and everything that was private isn't anymore. Lives are inside out, histories are, everybody has a confession.

We make our own order.

I had what could be rescued from an island smashed to pieces: A cat named Sterling. My little brother's stories. My mother's past. Old Carmen's trust. Deni at North and Eva, who would open her eyes in a day or two. Eva, who would not vanish. I had—now, new—a half sister named Gillian and a half brother named Johnny and pictures of my mother, young—pictures that I'd never seen and would never have seen if my aunt hadn't sent her children back to Haven.

Only thing in this world isn't replaceable is people.
Find your family.

Gillian and I spent a long time looking, a long time crying, a long time wondering what could be next, until finally we slipped the photos inside the box where they'd been stowed, and stood. We put some capsules of sand inside there, too, my mother's favorite bracelet, the smallest ceramic lady. We went hand under hand down Rapunzel, the continental shelf of the deck shifting above our heads and the attic creaking on its stilts. We had Sarah with us, my aunt's last pet, painted like no monster of the sea.

We had each other. Take away the half.

It would be another thirty-six hours before the Coast Guard would come. Before the bulldozers and the Porta-Potties, the medics, the Red Cross, the soup kitchens, the planners, the Humvees, the governor, the president—everything and everyone coming on barges, and no private boats allowed. Help came, and with the help came rules.

It would be two days before the news on Old Carmen's radio shifted to something new—epistles, that's what we called them. Messages from the mainland to the people stranded on Haven. Messages of love, and hope.

Rahna, there is room for you.

Cammy Vaughn, we send our love.

Mr. Friedley here. Mr. Friedley on Main. O'Six-
teens, send up a signal. Tell us how you are.

Ms. Isabel, I thought. He doesn't know yet. Mr. Friedley left the island. He doesn't know.

And then one hour in an early morning, the radio on Old Carmen's rock was talking straight to me:

Mira Banul, it said. *This is your mother and your brother. We're fine. We're really fine. We will find our way to you.*

I picked up Sterling. I held her close. I raised her paw and started weeping. And then I stood on Old Carmen's rock and waved as wide and high and hard as anybody would.

"He's alive," I said, "my little brother," and Gillian, who was there for good, who was family, who was part of me and part of Mickey, stood up on that rock and waved, a long, slow, heartbreaking wave that was also a goodbye to Johnny. She said she thought she could see Mickey and Jasper Lee in the distance. She thought she could see her brother.

"Prettiest part of the sky," she said. "That's Johnny."

"Yeah," I said. "I see him."

She took my hand. She held it.

There was no half between us.

Family.

8.

Eva opened her eyes, I was there. I saw. We were telling her stories about Haven. Old Carmen and the crabs she caught and how the meat was fire-roasted sweet. Cinnamon Nose and his peg-legged walk and the cat that I'd named Sterling. We told her about Deni's mom and the brigade and the meals they made, about Andra to the rescue, about Dr. Edwards, whose hair had gone white in the wink of so much ruin, and who was reading every book he'd salvaged.

Someone had found the picnic table with our mothers' Cupid arrows carved into it. Alabaster was standing straight with a six-foot water line. Kites were flying, built and rippling out of crazy, weird, wild things, and a little girl was dancing around with a pair of glitter wings. The sand was the streets and the streets were the sand and you could pull a sled down Main, and there was good news everywhere: people getting found, birds getting free, a spotted fawn and a bright white swan down by the sanctuary.

We didn't talk about Ms. Isabel.

We didn't say *lost*.

We said nothing about Gillian or the boy named Johnny Carpenter. About the regrets that were coming fast, or the past we could not fix.

We kept it whole. We kept it simple. That was the plan, our way of shoring Eva up. We talked about our Project Flows and how much more we'd have to say when we wrote our books for the future.

"Open your eyes, Eva," we said, until finally she did. They were bluer than the sea in the shining of the sun, bluer than a bucket. They were blue, and Eva was ours, and some things cannot be stolen.

9.

She told her story slow, in twisted pieces, but only after a while.
Only after we'd held her head so she could drink, the tiniest
sips—nutrition overseen by First Aid Andra.

Give her time, Andra had said.

Ask for nothing.

Wait.

Cinnamon Nose was lying beneath Eva's table-for-a-
bed, keeping her safe and protected. Sterling was curled in
my arms; I'd brought her with me. I'd left Gillian to fish
the seas beside Old Carmen, where, earlier in the day, we
could see the help coming in the distance—a fleet of boats,
a barge of provisions, a bridge of human beings—mainland
to Haven. Soon again and forever Haven would change.
Our brigades would change, our makeshift everythings,
the way we kept time by the sun. Old Carmen's rock would
become just a rock. Her fires would get smaller. People
who didn't know any better wouldn't know who she was. In
time there'd be water without salt and toilets that actually

flushed and shelters with roofs that weren't stars and meals that weren't scraped up from a wreck or the sea and no sling on Deni's arm. There'd be power and machines and trash trucks and Humvees. There'd be civil servants and private guards. There'd be the governor of the state, TV anchors, and TVs. There'd be the people we loved returning and the people we'd lost remembered, and Vacationeers threatening to join us, and next year, when the time was right, The Season, the O'Sixteens would come together to build again a sanctuary Ms. Isabel would have loved, a sanctuary suited to a great blue heron and all other perfect birds. Everything would change soon. Everything was on the verge, and everyone was everywhere, getting ready. Everyone except for Eva and Deni and me, three best friends forever.

"It's my fault," Eva said, her voice so small.

We thought she was confused, still dizzy. We asked for nothing, waited. We brought water to her lips, and then a cup of warm bouillon. Sustenance, a little at a time. Nothing hard to swallow.

"You don't have to talk," Deni told her.

"I want to," Eva said, her voice so crinkled and her heart so broken. She closed her eyes and went so deeply still that we thought we had lost her again.

It was a story. Eva's story. It came forward twisted. Shift and Eva. Eva and Shift. When the storm began, she said, she was alone. When the storm got worse, she called his phone. Told him to meet her out by the lighthouse, that she wanted to show him the world, that he had lost something, that she could give something back, that Eva, with her eyes, could show him.

"Unvanishing," she said.

Unvanishing.

It was hard to follow. It wasn't making sense. We let her talk. Let her ride the stories around in circles, show us what she really meant, which is that she loved this boy, believed in him, could see beyond the shadows of his hoodie. As if she had known him all her life, Eva said, and then a tear broke from her eye, and it stayed there, on her face, until Deni wiped it dry.

"You don't—" Deni said again.

"No," Eva said. "I do."

Out in the distance help was on its way. We could hear shouting from the shore, horns on the boats, scatterings of applause, loud jewelry ringing. But in triage it was just the three of us, and our Cinnamon Nose and our Sterling. Eva was trying so hard to talk. We told her to rest. She wouldn't.

"They said the storm was blowing out to sea," she started again, a bare whisper. "They said it, didn't they, Deni?"

"Shhhh," Deni said. "They did."

She closed her eyes, and I imagined—Eva and Shift by the lighthouse and the storm blowing in, the wind in Eva's hair. They must have stayed out there late, must have planned to stay all night. It was Eva's choice. Not his. Maybe she was telling him things about the cities out there—lost and buried, sea and time, Atlantis and Port Royal. Maybe he was telling her something, too, or looking through her binoculars, but I'll never know, because Shift was gone. Shift *is* gone. Eva said it. Then she closed her eyes and sobbed. There was no middle to her story. There was just wind, coming from nowhere, wind that knocked a lantern down, knocked Shift down, that's what Eva was saying, trying to say; it was so hard to understand.

"What is it, Eva?" Deni finally asked.

"Knocked," Eva whispered. "To the sea. I was standing right beside him."

She said other things after that, but they, too, were hard to follow. The bang of a fallen lantern against Shift's head. The boy unconscious and falling. The sea right there, below the cliff where the two of them had been standing. And then Eva herself was jumping in, but the sea was growing stronger. It was knocking Eva around with its strength, and Shift was already dead.

I thought of the starfish leg, the pale fishbones, the knots in Eva's hair. I thought of the waves crashing and her bones snapping, and I didn't know how she'd saved herself, how she was still here, with us.

"You went after him?" Deni said. "In the sea? In the storm?"

"You would have done it, too," Eva said. To Deni, and to me. "You would have."

And she was right.

She was crying harder, saddest sound I ever heard. I let Sterling to the ground and hugged Eva tight. Deni leaned in, too, the exact same time, and we were invisible cities and sea monsters and each of us shoring the other one up.

"Johnny Carpenter," Eva said. "I lost him."

And that's when I understood it worse than I had.

When all the pieces fit.

When I understood who Johnny was—the shift he'd brought to us.

10.

I thought the waves would rise up, toss down, rinse clean, and that I would still be standing here, solid.

I thought I knew all the monsters of the sea, but there are not words enough for naming.

I thought I knew what family was, but it fits no category.

I was wrong about almost everything, and some things: They do crumble.

Still:

We are here.

We are Year-Round.

We are rebuilding Haven.

We are remembering.

acknowledgments

Tamra Tuller, we love the sea, we live through storms, we are like sisters, like family. Thank you. Taylor Norman, you are a dear and necessary part of the process—careful, witty, diligent, and utterly there when I need you. Ginee Seo, for the conversations and the faith, for the words, I thank you. Sally Kim, Jaime Wong, Lara Morris Starr, Jennifer Tolo Pierce, Daria Harper, Jen Graham, Claire Fletcher, and Marie Oishi, you do your jobs so reliably well, and I am grateful. Debbie DeFord Minerva, copyeditor supreme and friend, you bent your ear toward my odd rhythms and you improved them. Thank you.

Amy Rennert: You always know when to call and what matters most. I'm grateful.

Stephen Fried, Nancy Bowden, Tom Boulden, Jessica Shoffel, and Deborah C. Whitcraft of the NJ Maritime Museum—thank you for telling me your storm stories.

Sean Banul: I gave Mira your last name with your permission. Every time I typed those five letters, I thought of your convictions and strength, of your cat with its hopeful paw raised. Reverend Agnes Norfleet: Deni's steadfast wisdom is inspired by you. Many others will find their names in these pages, and none of that is accidental. The community of us in the story of us.

Alyson Hagy, Rahna Reiko Rizzuto, Kelly Simmons, and Cyndi Reeves, thank you for the conversations along the way. A.S. King, Debbie Levy, and Ruta Sepetys, my thanks for all you are. Great gratitude as well to the teachers and the librarians and the book-sellers and the bloggers who find or make homes for the stories we write. Special thanks to Sister Kimberly Miller and her Little Flowers, who have honored me with their faith in the stories I write. The list is long. The heart is full.

Finally, and always, my son, Jeremy, who loves the beach as I love the beach and who cares about the work I do, and my husband, Bill, who joined me by the seaside during those off-seasons of near and lovely isolation.

Among the books I read while writing this book: *Surviving Sandy: Long Beach Island and the Greatest Storm of the Jersey Shore* by Scott Mazzella, Foreword by Margaret Thomas Buchholz, Introduction by Larry Savadove; *Great Storms of the Jersey Shore* by Larry Savadove and Margaret Thomas Buchholz, Foreword by Senator Bill Bradley; *Sandy: The Jersey Shore in the Eye of the Storm* presented by the *Asbury Park Press*; *The Rising Sea* by Orrin H. Pilkey and Rob Young; *The Global Warming Reader: A Century of Writing about Climate Change* edited by Bill McKibben; *The Sixth Extinction: An Unnatural History* by Elizabeth Kolbert; *Field Notes from a Catastrophe: Man, Nature, and Climate Change* by Elizabeth Kolbert; *A Grain of Sand: Nature's Secret Wonder* by Dr. Gary Greenberg, Foreword by Stacy Keach; and *The Book of Barely Imagined Beings: A 21st Century Bestiary* by Caspar Henderson.

For more information about Hunter syndrome and other rare disorders, please visit the National Organization for Rare Disorders (NORD): https://rarediseases.org and Saving Case & Friends: https://savingcase.com.